The Absent Woman

The Absent Woman

Marlene Lee

For Alice and Bill, Loyal friends and supporters.

Marlene

Holland House

www.hhousebooks.com

Copyright © 2013 by Marlene Lee

Marlene Lee asserts her moral right to be identified as the author of this book

All rights reserved. This book or any portion thereof may not be reproduced or used in any manner whatsoever without the express written permission of the publisher except for the use of brief quotations in a book review.

All characters appearing in this work are fictitious. Any resemblance to real persons, living or dead, is purely coincidental.

Hardback ISBN 978-1-909374-40-9
Paperback ISBN 978-1-909374-41-6
Kindle ISBN 978-1-909374-42-3
Epub 978-1-909374-43-0

Cover design by Ken Dawson

Published in the USA and UK

Holland House Books
Holland House
47 Greenham Road
Newbury
Berkshire
RG14 7HY
United Kingdom

www.hhousebooks.com

For Andrew, Maurice,
Yuko, Marisa, and
the children

Acknowledgements

I wish to thank Ella Leffland, writer, friend, and inspiration; Holland House Books and Robert Peett, the best publisher and editor one could ask for; New York State Summer Writers' Institute for a long period of incubation; Brooklyn College Writing Program for the frosting on the cake; and my beloved sister and first reader, Lavetta McCune. Vincent, I remember your loving heart. Finally, to all the friends and colleagues who have helped me, I can only say thank you again.

1

"She collected starfish?"

"Starfish, shells—"

I imagined sour-mud-and-vegetable smells at low water; I didn't want rooms that smelled like a tide pool.

"—and rocks and feathers," he said. "You name it, she collected it." Specimens ascended the old staircase in an unbroken line of flora and fauna.

"Do you want to go up?" he asked, pulling a key from his pocket. He looked well-off, dressed in tailored slacks and cardigan. Not the type to mess about with broken-down Victorian buildings. Probably waiting for a developer. Or maybe he *was* the developer.

"No. No, thanks," I answered, backing away from the beveled glass door at street level. "It's not what I had in mind."

"Pretty lonely," he admitted as we walked through the vacant lot between the abandoned hotel and the hardware store. In back, a spindly fire escape staggered up the old brick flank. Someone, probably the starfish collector, had hung red curtains at the windows.

"You're not from around here, are you?" he asked.

"Seattle"

"And you want to move up here?"

"I'm seriously considering it."

"Why Hilliard?"

"I like the town. It's—on the edge of something. You know, before you get to the islands."

He laughed politely.

Behind the hotel we pushed through died-back weeds and remnants of a concrete foundation, viewing his tall, narrow, derelict building from all sides.

"You sure you don't want to go inside?" I surveyed once more the aged brick facade, weathered cornices, the rippled glass in the high, old windows.

"I'm sure," I said.

The landlord unlocked his Buick. "What was it you said you were doing up here?" he asked, one foot in the car.

"A three-month project," I said. He looked at me one last time and drove away. I stood for a moment in his exhaust and contemplated the street and my answer, both empty. If only there *was* a three-month project. And if only the vague dissatisfaction I felt could actually be cured in three months. I needed something to devote myself to. Something that takes a lifetime to work on. A hobby that becomes an obsession. Seashells, rocks, and dried flowers assembled in a scientifically labeled procession up an endless flight of stairs. Great Books. Piano lessons. World peace.

How could I tell people who exclaimed, "Surely you didn't leave your husband and children for a *hobby!*" that I had a passion to become passionate about something? That I felt buried in deadening comfort? How could I say out loud that marriage and family life bored me?

I bought a paper at the corner tavern and began climbing High Street. At a stoplight, I turned and looked back toward the water. Hilliard sloped uphill from the bay. Below me, rough docks led to commercial fishing boats. Around the curving shoreline, a well-maintained marina served pleasure craft. Above it all, casting an aloof, disinterested shadow over the harbor and town, a mountainous crag patrolled the little world. In Europe there would have been a castle on top, enduring slashing rains, disfiguring fogs, summer heat through the centuries. But here in Hilliard, instead of a castle, were handsome Victorian houses built by sea captains and boat manufacturers in the last century.

The light changed. Three blocks up I stopped at Mom's Restaurant, windows filled with ornamental food that might fade but never rot: wax apples, peppers, eggplant, and plastic grapes that swayed above commemorative plates. My ex-husband and sons would hate this place. Inside, under a doily anchored by a spotted-cow cream pitcher, I found a table. A gray-haired waitress plodded toward me. She smiled tiredly, possibly sapped by so much decoration.

"Coffee and toast," I said. On her next slow pass through the diner I held out my cup.

"Cold today," she observed.

I nodded and studied the cream pitcher. "Is there a trick to this?"

She picked up the cow, sighed, and shot a stream of milk into my coffee. "New In Hilliard?"

"Just visiting."

She glanced at the paper lying open to the classifieds.

"I may be moving here," I added.

"Where you from?"

"Seattle."

She fiddled with her hairnet. "Why would you want to move up here?"

"I've always liked Hilliard" was all I said. "The ferry, the fishing boats, the"

"You probably need a rest," she offered. "Boy, I know I could use one."

"That's it," I agreed. "I need a rest."

2

"I FEEL FLAT," I tried to explain to my friend Jerry the day after I'd seen the old hotel. "I want adventure. I want to accomplish something. I want to live in a fishing village at the edge of the continent. Make mistakes and recover from them. Depend on myself. See what I can do."

Jerry's laugh was without amusement. "No one leaves their husband, their kids, their job because of *flatness*. That's self-indulgent, Virginia. Adolescent. A luxury most of us cannot afford."

"Well, maybe it's a luxury you don't *choose* to afford," I replied. We'd been watching the late news at my house, the small 1930s bungalow Ron and I had bought as a rental before the children were born. Jerry spent one night a week with me there, beginning to settle in; I had begun to feel I was merely settling.

He pulled away. "You throw away one blessing after another, don't you?"

I'd never heard him use the word 'blessing'. It clashed with his style: always smooth, always current. The word must have come from a childhood saturated in church attendance. Baptist, maybe. I stood up from the sofa.

"Why did you get married in the first place?"

"I was trying to do all the right things," I flared. "I loved Ron. I thought I was supposed to get married."

"You're a good-looking woman," he continued. "You went to college."

"Two years."

"You're a terrific piano-player. You have two wonderful kids. What is your problem?"

I had no answer.

"Why don't you go back to school or something if you're bored?"

"I went to court reporting school," I said, proud of at least that decision. "I'm a court reporter."

"Maybe you should have gone to law school."

I'd considered it. But I'd been afraid to compete.

"It would have been a better-paid adventure," he added. "A better-paid blessing." He paused and overcame what I saw in his eyes: the wish to hurt me. "Why don't you relax and—enjoy yourself?"

The fight went out of both of us, but there was no rising sap to take its place. There never had been much rising sap between us. After a few more words and ragged silences he went to the closet for his raincoat, stepped out onto the porch, and snapped open his umbrella. A gust of wind spattered the windows. His lean, crisp body, protected from weather by clothing made from lamb's wool and sold through high-end catalogs with addresses in the Pacific Northwest islands, was too perfect. He could have been a male model in one of those catalogs, lounging near a woodburning stove, wearing the perfect flannel shirt. His loafers had tassels. I didn't like those tassels nor the fact that he never forgot his umbrella.

He turned on his heel and walked to the street. As he drove away in his BMW, I stood at the edge of the dark porch and let the rain dampen my hair and face. I didn't mind the rain. I didn't mind that the four-month relationship was over.

3

MY SONS LIVED WITH THEIR FATHER in a drafty Victorian house we'd bought ten years earlier, not far from the university: a house whose high-ceilinged rooms and wainscoted walls had heard little honest talk between Ron and me. Once when the children were eight and nine I expressed a thought I'd always been careful to contain.

"My life is flat," I said to Ron. "I think I was created to do something wonderful, but I'm not doing it."

"Matt and Phil and I aren't wonderful enough for you?"

"It's not that. You have your teaching, and the boys don't need me as much as they used to."

"That's what you said before you became a court reporter, Virginia. I agreed to your going back to school. You did it. Now you're a court reporter. Isn't that enough?"

"It's good, but—"

"You bet it's good." Before he stepped into his study he looked me in the eye. "What do you really want, Virginia?" He turned and shut the door behind him. Through the transom I heard the clicking of the computer keyboard.

It wasn't that I wanted to be a dissatisfied person or an emotional hypochondriac. I wanted to be fulfilled by my family and job and I was ashamed of my self-centered ambitions. Ashamed of my longing for something more. Still, the yearning grew like a weed, and the weed put out large, glossy leaves that began to crowd out the smaller, tamer plants Ron and I were tending. We tried to ignore it, tossing there at the edge of the garden, choking out pleasure and blocking the light, as if it had sprouted from a seed dropped by a bad bird. But it would not wither or die back. It grew like a beanstalk.

A year and a half later, I climbed it.

"I have to leave!" I cried on our last night together. "I can't go through the motions anymore!"

He struck the headboard with his fist. "Then go! But the boys stay with me!"

At the top of the beanstalk I reached, not fulfillment, but a world of anxiety.

4

I PULLED UP IN THE DRIVEWAY for my Wednesday-night dinner with the boys, feeling, as always, disoriented when I looked at the steps and sidewalk I'd swept for years. The giant potted jade, still watered regularly, flourished without me.

I set the brake and waited in the car for a moment, trying to pretend I didn't remember the kitchen curtains, the front door latch, the way the daylight touched the boys' faces when I woke them for school.

I stepped up onto the porch and rang the bell. Matt and Lawrence came to the door in their soccer uniforms.

"Did I miss a game?" I asked, digging in my purse for the soccer schedule.

"No. We got our uniforms today," said Matt.

Ron came up behind them. "Out of the uniforms, boys."

"But can't we wear them to dinner?" They turned the question to me.

"You look terrific, but do what your dad says."

The boys went upstairs to change clothes.

"I've got a lecture to finish," Ron said.

"Night class this semester?"

He nodded abruptly and turned toward his study off the hall. The front door remained open. Standing there, surrounded by damp cement smell of porch, it occurred to me it really didn't matter where I lived: I was either in or out of this house. Lights came on in the upstairs bedroom. The boys would be dropping their soccer clothes on the floor about now. A neighbor's dog barked in the dusk. Ron's hedge clippers lay under the Douglas fir; it wasn't like him to leave something out in weather.

An impulse seized me and I stuck my head into the empty hallway. "Can I take all of you to dinner?" It was my night with the children, but who was to say we all couldn't eat together now and then?

"I'm busy," Ron replied from his study.

"Pizza!" shouted Lawrence, running downstairs.

"Hamburgers!" cried Matt from the landing.

"We'll discuss it," I said, edging backwards off the porch. To Ron I called out, "I'll have them back by bedtime." The boys spilled from the house around me, running ahead to the car and plunging in, one in front, one in back. Tonight they didn't fight over who would sit where. But since they couldn't agree on the kind of food they wanted, I decided for them.

"We'll eat at the Mexican restaurant on the Avenue." I ruffled Lawrence's hair and turned to look into the eyes of Matthew a fraction of a second before he glanced away. Lawrence bent toward the console and turned on the radio. While they listened to a rock group, honing their tastes for adolescence, my thoughts drifted back to Hilliard—shoreline, docks, steep rock without castle—and came to rest on an old hotel with starfish-studded steps and bright red curtains at the windows.

"We have to be back in time to watch 'Wonders of Science' with Dad," said Matt.

"Yeah," said Lawrence. "Tonight it's dinosaurs."

"What time does it start?"

"Eight-thirty."

"We'll make a point of it." I sounded cheerful, but a pang of loneliness penetrated the thin protection I'd grown since the divorce.

"Tyrannosaurus rex?" I asked. "Remember the library books

we read when you were little? Tyrannosaurus rex, stegosaurus, brachiosaurus . . ."

"Those books weren't scientific," Matt said critically.

"The program isn't for kids," Lawrence said.

"Still, I liked the books," I insisted, at the moment unable to remember the pleasure. "The pictures were nice. At the time, you liked them, too."

I drove up and down the steep hills of my former Queen Anne neighborhood while the abandoned hotel insinuated itself into my thoughts. I looked at the clock, the speedometer, the gas gauge, in an effort to be practical. The rock group was screaming *"You! You! Yes! You! You!"* Even assuming it was a plan, not a daydream, why should I consider a broken-down hotel for a temporary home? At the least, it would draw the contempt of Ron and the kids, and confirm their opinion and my suspicion: something is wrong with Mother.

"We're playing East Hill," Matthew yelled above the radio.

"When is that?" I yelled back.

"Saturday!"

"Could we turn the music down?" I asked. Lawrence lowered the volume.

"I want to discuss something with you," I said, not planning to say that at all. But why wait till dinner, a stage with a stage setting, forks and knives for props, the table to put the elbows on? "You two know life changes, don't you?" I began awkwardly. "Already you know that, right?"

Stillness and silence from the boys.

"I'm thinking of staying in a town called Hilliard. It's sixty miles north of here," I said. "For a while."

"You're moving?" Lawrence asked, shocked.

"Not for very long. Just three months. I'll still see you twice a week."

"Three months?" Matt said. "Did you tell Dad?"

"Not yet. I want your opinion first."

Matt reached between the bucket seats and turned up the radio. Rock music rolled over us again, urban and distressed. The boys withdrew into themselves, I withdrew into myself, and here we all were, apart and withdrawn on one of our few evenings together. God, I wondered, how long does it take for divorce to be final? Again, in spite of myself, I was climbing the hotel steps cluttered with remnants of nature. Now I wanted to see the rooms upstairs. What else had the starfish woman done besides hang red curtains at the windows?

In front of a sidewalk flower shop I pulled the car over to the curb and turned off the ignition. Blood-red and rust-colored chrysanthemums stood in tubs of water; it was autumn, the short-lived golden season. I rested my left arm on the steering wheel and turned to the boys.

"Since the divorce I don't know how I'm supposed to live." They sat still, embarrassed and curious. "I feel there's something I'm supposed to be doing, but I don't know what it is."

"Like what?" asked Lawrence, fiddling with the radio dial, knowing it wouldn't come on without the ignition.

"I'm not sure. Maybe something hard, or maybe something simple that I haven't paid enough attention to." They looked puzzled. "Maybe a change of scenery will help." I thought of a comparison: "Like Dad's sabbaticals."

"But he teaches college!"

"So? I'm a court reporter!" Irritation felt blissfully ordinary. "If you tell me you don't want me to go, I'll think harder about it."

"If you want to do it, go ahead," said Matt after a long silence.

"Yeah," said Lawrence. "You will, anyway."

At dinner we talked about school, their soccer teams. I asked about the neighborhood kids I'd known from years of carpools and birthday parties. But gradually we stopped talking. On the way home they moved away from me; turned their heads toward the windows of the car; diligently studied the stores along the avenue, the apartment buildings, and finally the turn-of-the-century houses of Queen Anne Hill. When the car stopped in the driveway they gave me a perfunctory kiss and rushed away. Their father was home. He would always be there.

I drove through the dark, hilly streets of Seattle to my small house in Magnolia filled with books and deposition transcripts, the piano, photograph albums of the children and Ron when we had all appeared happy together. And maybe that's what happiness is, I thought wryly as I threw my coat on a chair. If things appear happy, maybe they are.

I poured myself a glass of wine and saw again the old hotel looming over the channel. When I turned on the lamp, the dark wood of the baby-grand piano glowed. Black and white keys seemed attached to a nervous system: my own. From the music rack, notes and staves of a Chopin etude throbbed on the page. I sat down and began to play. As phrases took shape, an old building emerged above the notes: it stood beside a channel, and starfish steps led to dark, unknown rooms, and brave red curtains hung at the windows.

5

"I CAN DEFINITELY AFFORD TO DO IT," I told Denise as we sat proofreading transcript at our desks. "With my own house rented out, I'll survive. For three months, anyway."

"Three months? Are you sure you can live up there alone for three months?"

"Pretty sure."

"Why?" she asked, lifting the shoulders of her well-cut suit.

"I need a rest."

"But you don't look tired." The telephone rang. It was Jerry. I took it in the coffee room.

"Are they all fishermen up there in Hilliard, or what?" he asked.

"No, they don't seem to be. Why are you calling?"

"What does the town look like?"

"A lot of boats. A boatyard. The docks."

"The town isn't making it, Virginia. The big ferry doesn't come there anymore."

"That's right."

"Why are you moving?"

I began to realize how much my independence disturbed him. "I've told you there's something I need to learn. The little voice. There comes a time when you have to listen to it. Find out if it can be trusted. One last chance before—"

"What's the real reason, Virginia?"

"The kids belong to Ron!" I shot back. He'd pressed me. He wasn't important anymore, so I told him the truth. "They don't need me!"

"You got rid of your family, remember?" The malice transmitted well over the phone line.

"Rubbish!" I snapped. "I'm still close to the children. Ron and I worked it out."

"And your piano," Jerry said, taking another tack. "Didn't he buy you the piano?"

"Yes." I was ashamed of the ugly, poignant truth: I'd ended up loving the piano more than I loved Ron. I shared my life with shining gold pedals, bouncing hammers, an upholstered bench. Scrambling to change the subject, I said, "People live out of habit. I don't want to walk through a part."

"Isn't that what life's all about? You walk through your part as well as you can?"

"You write your part as you go along!" I said. Jerry was no more adept at fifty-year marriages than I was: he was forty-four and unmarried. If he expected to have a golden anniversary, he'd have to take good care of himself and live to a hundred.

"Have you ever considered seeing a psychiatrist?" he asked.

"When I left Ron he said the same thing."

There was a smug silence, then dry, rapid speech. "Keep it under control, Virginia," he said, and hung up.

The phone call had been a postscript to our final quarrel the week before. The small step I'd taken, merely driving to Hilliard for a day, had changed things more than I'd expected.

6

Late Sunday afternoon I sat at my kitchen table watching a brilliant, fitful sunset over the Sound. Black clouds raced above the ridge to the west. I'd always associated cloud-watching with serenity, but these were traveling fast, and it wasn't a pleasant, easy sky. Everything seemed in movement, with the deep red light breaking through thunderheads and the wind hurling the first big drops of a rainstorm at the kitchen windows. The sun dropped into the Sound. Its absence stained the edge of the sky.

I turned on the lamp and began playing a Bach two-part invention, carefully at first, staying on the surface of the music until the drive and momentum of the theme plunged me deeper. The bass, when it carried the melody, resonated like a confident, rested man. The treble soared like a woman, soothing, then decisive, finally exciting. Under and around the notes I added my own theme to Bach's, singing it out through my fingers: What happens to children whose mothers go away for a while? What happens to the mothers?

Two days later I returned to Hilliard. "How long has she been gone?" I asked the owner of the hotel, keeping to the center of each stair, well away from the specimens.

"A few weeks," he replied.

"Why did she leave?"

The man shrugged. "She didn't give a reason. Said she'd be back before summer, and if I'd hold the apartment for her I could rent it out with her furniture in it."

'Furniture' was not quite the word. A card table in the kitchen, one overstuffed chair of questionable vintage and cleanliness in the middle room, a rickety table and one straight chair in what was—must be—a studio of some kind. A twin bed neatly made up in a small room overlooking the street.

I stopped at a window facing the channel. Below me, the little ferry to Guemes Island held eight cars, its maximum load. Rounding Hilliard Point, a sailboat ran with the wind. I lifted my eyes and felt like a bird flying toward Cypress Island and the islands beyond: Orcas, Lummi, Lopez, Shaw.

"I don't believe it," I heard the landlord say from the studio. I found him standing between a table and straight chair shaking his head. "She decorated everything, didn't she?" Fabric cut-outs and paper constructions hung, flew, and fluttered all about us. I ducked under a piñata. Mermaids with yarn for hair draped themselves across one wall, wearing netting to cover their breasts and fins. They looked at me with cheerful, stitched eyes. Stretched against the width of the west wall, a piece of blue corduroy—gathered, smocked, and pocketed—held a collection of serendipitous cards, photographs, a red-brown maple leaf, a stone, a twig with dried berries still hanging on.

In the bedroom a bamboo clothes rod had been strung up with rope from ceiling hooks. I studied what she'd left behind: overalls, two plaid flannel shirts, one cotton blouse, sweatshirt, jacket with hood. The clothes were clean and hung in an orderly fashion.

"Does she keep in touch with you?" I asked, wondering if she planned to come back and check on who—if anyone—was living in her rooms.

"She wrote me a postcard from Kansas. Some little town."

A splendid memory shot through my mind, a memory of summer in Kansas with my mother. Harvest time, and we sat beside my grandma shelling peas over a tin dishpan.

"I'll take it until she comes back," I said impulsively, and wrote out a check. The landlord and I climbed downstairs, sidestepping the specimens. He closed the beveled glass door behind him and locked it with a large key.

"This is yours," he said. I opened my hand. The key was heavy and cold. The kind of key, I thought as I got in my car, that leaves your hand smelling metallic. If you sweat, it will rust on your skin.

A storm was gathering as I drove south on the highway. Wet wind coming off grass and dirt smelled sweet, then rank. In the fields, pulsating arcs of liquid manure sprayed the crops, mixing brownly with the rain that finally hit, enriching the soil for—I didn't know what. Out there, beyond the windshield wipers and the sheet of water flowing down the glass, something was growing. It wasn't wheat; this is dairy country. I'd heard the term 'green feed'. Maybe in the coffee shop at the junction I could find someone who would tell me what was planted in these fields.

7

"I'm going to do it, Ross," I said one week before the end of the month. "I'm ready for that leave of absence."

He shook his head and thrust out his chin, raking the raw, shaved skin of his neck against his starched collar. Everything about Ross Wyler was tight: collar, belt, jaw, brain. We reporters, so-called independent contractors to his court reporting agency, were on a short leash.

"It's a romantic idea," he said critically, massaging one chapped nostril with the tip of his index finger. Ross almost always had a cold or allergy. Considering the tight hold he had on his environment, he was surprisingly unwell.

"I can afford to go if there's still a job here when I get back," I said. Whenever I talked to Ross I sounded argumentative. He didn't like dissenters and wanted silent, self-employed reporters he could treat as employees. It was a lucrative business for a middle man, eyed from the distance by the IRS. The attorney socked it to the client, we socked it to the attorney, Ross socked it to us, and everyone lived off the fruits of dispute, dissension, and dissolution.

"Don't stay away too long, Virginia," he warned. "I won't wait forever. You're not indispensable."

8

AFTER SEVERAL ATTEMPTS, one of the split logs ignited, the flame smoked, and the tin stovepipe began to creak and warm. I swept ashes from the cracked linoleum, put them in a bucket I found under the sink, and set it on the outside landing.

A cold, watery wind came off the Sound. Below me half a block west sat a long, one-story frame building: 'Padilla Bay Lumber' it said in evenly spaced letters above the loading dock. A graceful dory rested in a scaffolding of two-by-fours at the front entrance. Beyond the lumber company, several old Victorian homes gazed down on the channel. I faced north and saw Cypress Island, its steep, wooded hillside rising sharply out of the water. Beyond, Orcas Island was a blue-gray blur, a mountain peak lost in cloud cover. I returned to the kitchen and acquainted myself with the contents of cupboards: crazed but pretty plates and cups, saucers and bowls. Not a matched set in the place. Still, a comfortable, flowered jumble. The shelves were clean enough, and the floors were clean enough, and I wasn't in Hilliard to clean or pass inspection of any kind.

But it was hard not to stand at attention to myself. I should be proofreading, practicing scales, improving my mind, volunteering for the less fortunate. Looking about me, I realized I *was* the less fortunate. Poor rooms in a deserted old hotel, and electric heat in the middle room only. Dead starfish underfoot each time I made my way up the double flight of stairs with a sackful of groceries, climbing slowly, the sound of my footsteps echoing in the chipped, high-ceilinged spaces.

Hilliard had grown away from the channel. Its malls, fast food franchises, and auto parts stores were uphill and south of me; south of my hotel; south of the long-defunct cannery whose gray, ramshackle buildings were falling in on themselves, pilings broken off like bad teeth; south of the old hardware store with its pine plank floor, office behind a wire mesh cage, inventory in heavy wooden drawers; south of the boatyard.

I made the bed with sheets and blankets from home. Across High Street, behind the low Bar Fly Tavern, they were building a boat—no, a ship. A vast skeleton of a vessel in the boatyard, with the dark, muffled sky showing through its ribs. Like the little dory west of me, it rested in a knocked-together support, an enormous cradle to hold its outward-bowing sides and keel bottom upright. A boom carrying a man in a bucket slowly moved along one of the ribs and the welding machine started up, the engine whined hard, the arc snapped, sparks fell.

I watched the man weld steel to steel and tack rib to keel. Then the boom lifted him to the level of the deck and I heard the welding machine go under its load. Again the arc snapped. Again sparks showered. I watched it over and over, imagining the burnt smell of shorted-out electricity.

As far as I knew, Matthew and Lawrence had never seen a boatyard. Maybe they could visit sooner than planned, and maybe they'd be as interested as I was in watching a ship being built.

Without children, friends, job, I vacillated between staying indoors or getting acquainted with the town.

"I'll do both," I said aloud. The words, my own voice, helped make the bedroom mine. I got up from the bed and hung my few items of clothing on hangers, making the bamboo pole sway on its ropes. Other than this make-shift wardrobe, the bed, and a small chest with three drawers, there was nothing else. Since I had no mirrors, perfume bottles, nor family photos, the ship across the way would be my bric-a-brac.

I hurried to the kitchen woodburner which by now needed another log. The woman had left a nice supply of firewood underneath the outside stairs. She probably split the logs herself, I decided.

The floorboard heaters in the living room were warming up. In an effort to save heat, I tacked a blanket above the doorway to the woman's studio. That's what I would call it: the absent woman's studio. I might be renting it, but it certainly wasn't mine. All the stuff on the walls and shelves was her work. I would live in the kitchen and living room. I would sleep in the bedroom.

I left to explore Hilliard. In a wedge-shaped, unpainted stucco building I found the only music store in town. The old proprietor wore a sweater and soft, worn slacks held up by suspenders. He moved slowly between second-hand records, second-hand books, and second-hand instruments.

"Do you have practice rooms?" I asked, removing my knit gloves. "Do you have a piano I could play once in a while?"

He shook his head, which looked a little like the slacks: soft and worn. His yellow-gray scalp puckered above the ears.

"No. You better go to Vernon."

I picked up a second-hand harmonica.

"You play one of those?"

"No," I said. "Just the piano."

"New in town?"

I nodded.

"Where you from?"

"Seattle."

"Where you living?"

I braced myself for a curious stare.

"An apartment," I said. "At the end of town."

"Not much down there except the hotel."

I remained silent.

"Living in the hotel, are you?"

I nodded again, challenged to lift my chin and show some pride.

"Why, there's a piano in that hotel, Missy. Did you know that?"

It was my turn to look interested. "Where?"

"Upstairs. Leastways it was there when I tuned it a few years back."

"What was it doing there?"

"Dunno. They was a teacher who played it. I guess she went someplace else." His voice died, then wheezed to life again. "Everybody goes someplace else." He paused for a cough. "Said she was a teacher, anyways. Looked like one."

"A piano teacher?"

"At one time."

"Do you know if she's lived there recently?"

"Don't think so." He climbed onto his high, three-legged stool behind the old cash register. "People come and go. It's a hotel."

I hurried back to my end of town, unlocked the door, and climbed the stairs. Instead of opening the kitchen door, entry to all my other rooms, I turned left at the newel post and worked my way down the long hall, throwing open closed doors.

The first room held mattresses, at least twenty mattresses piled on the floor. Chunks of ceiling plaster lay on the stained ticking. The next door was a bathroom, its long, claw-footed tub filthy. Then a cleaning closet. A door to a balcony that no longer existed. Farther down, a room filled with fishing net gathered into an enormous mesh pile soft as hair. Finally, at the end of the hall, a circular room hanging over the street corner; bay windows letting in blue-gray island light, daylight as pure as a flute note. On the far wall, pushed against yellowed, still-flowering wallpaper, an old upright piano. I drew in my breath, thrilled. But I feared its tone.

Someone had closed the serpentine lid over the keys. I rolled it back into the piano, lid of a slow eye, and touched middle C.

Clink. It clinked like a barroom piano. Which it probably was.

I heard the gyration in the note, the untuned, wobbly vibrato. I played a scale from C to the high notes, back down to the lows. Every key sounded.

As I walked back to my rooms, I marveled that the thing played at all after sitting in that damp, unheated hotel for years on end. I would have it tuned. I picked up a straight chair from the absent woman's studio and carried it back to the piano. With my jacket on, I sat down and played everything I knew by heart. The pedal didn't work. Schubert sounded disjointed, but I could make up the sweet legato in my head. Bach and Paradisi sounded good. I needed more of this kind of practice to strengthen my fingers and teach me the real shape of the piece. Like the steel ribs in the ship, the notes stood out cleanly, each one alone and noticeable. No damper to muffle and blur one sound into another.

But after I ran through my meager classical repertoire, I banged out some boogie-woogie. I'd always wanted to play popular music by ear: jazz, ragtime, musical theatre ("The hills are alive . . .") But I'd learned this boogie-woogie from sheet music. Every time I played it, I pretended it was the first time, and that I was pulling it out of the air; pulling it out of an abundant intuition and talent that sprang from deep within the artistic, musical personality I longed for.

9

In Hilliard there was nothing in the evenings and little in the daytimes but myself. I didn't have a television and I would be damned if I'd buy one. This is what I asked for: this is what I got.

I memorized the library hours and bought a season ticket to the concert series. And I began to walk. At first I walked straight uptown and straight back again. Then during my trips to the library and grocery store I began to explore the town, stringing out my walks into the early evening so that I passed lighted windows in houses. I saw families eating, watching television, quarreling, laughing, getting into cars, getting out of cars, bringing in bicycles, calling the dog. My destinations were vague, as vague as twilight, as soft and seductive as first nightfall. Stars on clear nights were holes puncturing a dark cloth, bright clues to something beyond. And a night of clouds was a moody, living presence, soft as a lover's breath, as intimate, as safe, and as kind. I could enfold myself in an undefined sense of the universe mixed with a sweet, pleasant sadness that was not quite desolation.

There were tonal variations: mornings were active, purposeful, even though my goal might be only to reach a certain street, turn a certain corner, identify the edge of town, or locate the restaurant with the best coffee or soup. Afternoons were full and slow and leisurely. In the evenings I felt sensuous and absolutely lonely.

I had thought I would spend most of my time on the beach along the channel, or up and down the docks. But in the first two weeks I seemed to crave town. I smiled at people who only half-smiled back. I was chatty with clerks. "I'm not an eccentric woman who lives alone in an old hotel," I wanted to say. "I'm more, much more. I earn my own money. I have a job to return to. I'm pretty and well-groomed, not too tall or short, not too fat or thin. I have two children. I used to go to PTA meetings. *I'm all right.*"

I was browsing in the biography shelves one day when a troop of preschoolers tramped through the library toward the children's section, their shouts and calls decorated with '*ssh's*' from two teachers at the head of the line and a mother bringing up the rear. With a book under one arm I followed them to their story hour as if, there, I might find two little guys who were mine. While they deployed on the carpet and tried mastering their arms and legs, one boy wearing bib overalls and little red tennis shoes wandered away from the group. He suddenly broke into a run toward the aquarium and, as I watched, tripped, fell hard, and hit a bookshelf. Blood smeared his forehead and the spines of picture books. I reached him first. I'd instinctively gathered him up in my arms when one of the women came rushing back, frightened by his screams. She saw the blood, grabbed him from me, and ran into the main reading room yelling for someone to call an ambulance. But not before she glared at me.

I followed her, calling out, "He tripped and hit his head!" She glanced at me again, a slice of eye movement, as if I were a danger. A siren wailed toward us. I thought she was overreacting. She and another adult, an onlooker like me, for instance, could have taken him to the emergency room where he probably needed only a few stitches.

The ambulance took them away, its siren gradually losing force down distant streets. I remained near the door, feeling humiliated. The reference librarian avoided my eyes.

"He fell," I repeated.

"Yes," she said, and returned to her file.

"I have children," I said.

She looked up.

"Two boys."

"How nice."

"They're eight and nine now."

Still looking at me, she got up from her desk and went through a doorway labeled 'Staff Only.' I retreated to the biography shelves and replaced my book. Then I walked home fast, ran up the stairs, and slammed the kitchen door behind me. At once I set about making a fire in the stove. When the blaze caught I stood in the middle of the room and folded my arms hard against my ribs. How dare anyone think I would hurt a child? How dare those women not recognize I was a mother, too? I could match them hour for hour at children's libraries.

I stomped into the bedroom, where I sat on the edge of the bed and watched the welder in the bucket stitch another rib to the keel. I watched and watched. A mother yet not a mother. A mother without children. Rib without keel. I went to the kitchen and began searching. The cupboards were a jumble. No cup and saucer matched. My attention flitted from dishes, to teakettle, to the window, and finally, to the world outside the window. I didn't know what I was searching for. Oncoming dusk flattened and darkened the water. Currents I couldn't see carved out the land; ate at the banks; flowed over crabs and eel grass.

I stood by the red curtains until night obscured everything but the lights of the little ferry slowly passing from one side of the channel to the other.

10

THE TOWER ROOM at the end of the hall became my music room. In spite of clammy walls and dark smell of old floorboards and molding, in the winter sunshine my circular room blazed. I placed a small electric heater near the piano bench while I practiced. Between pieces I moved it from place to place, creating temporary hot spots all around the room.

The old man in the sweater and suspenders came to tune the piano.

"She needs to be played, that's for sure," he said, striking a G, adding the octave, tightening the nut, and repeating the operation.

"I play her every day," I said. "But I need some new music. I've been working on the same old stuff for a long time."

His cataracts almost lit up. "Well, now, you want to come down to the shop." Later, when he had replaced his tools in the mildewed tuning kit, we descended the stairs, climbed into a panel truck marked 'Raithel's Music' and wheezed up High Street.

"We'll find some music for you," he assured me, unlocking the door and turning the 'Back Soon' sign that hung on a string. He took off his jacket, frozen shoulder joints grinding into action, then led me to a cabinet containing a jumble of music: Berlioz next to pop tunes from the '40s, Gilbert and Sullivan beside Ellington. I sorted through the shelf.

"She'll sound better now," he said, seating himself on the high stool. His suspenders drooped over his weak lungs.

"Yes," I said, "but a Steinway she is not."

He laughed, hacked, hawked, and repeated, "A Steinway she is not." When he'd recovered, I pulled out a thin book, *Early Beethoven Sonatas*, and brought it to the cash register.

"Some day I want to learn all of them."

"Do it now!" He pounded a spot over one lung. "Asbestosis. They said I couldn't work." He lifted an arm in a careful gesture to include all the people who had told him so. "That was ten years ago. And here I am. A lot of those fine doctors are dead."

"Do you know where the woman is who used to teach piano?" I asked as he totaled the charges on an old adding machine.

"Haven't heard of her for quite some time." He scratched his gray chin. "Used to teach there in the hotel."

"Does she have relatives in town?"

"Used to have a son. Fisherman, I think. Lived on a boat." The cash register rang, numbers popped up, and the drawer flew open. "She used to play organ for the Methodists. I'd ask at the church if I was you." I thanked him and said good-bye. In the midst of a phlegmy attack he managed to count out my change, close the drawer, and recross his legs. I hesitated, waiting to see that he didn't fall off the stool, but he motioned me on out as if to say, "I've been coughing for years and haven't slipped off yet."

The day was flat and overcast, gray-white, opaque. I knew it wouldn't last. The afternoon would more than likely bring a new and passionate geography to the sky: swollen clouds, ragged light. I tucked the music roll under one arm and began walking toward the Methodist Church.

Beethoven liked to walk, I'd read. I remembered an illustration from a biography showing him on a windy day in the Black Forest wearing untidy waistcoat and breeches, his hair standing out wildly from his large head. All his life he moved from place to place, house to house, rooms to rooms.

My music slipped and I stopped to tighten the roll, doubling the rubber band Mr. Raithel had snapped around the book.

Why do some people move and some people stay where they are? Why do some people have gnawings and others don't? Every person on the face of the earth should have a biographer. Someone who explains. How unfair that we should appear and disappear so quickly, without a trace. Better records should be kept on all of us.

The light at the intersection turned red. I shifted the roll of music to the other arm and crossed with the green. And why should a magnificent person like Beethoven have to die in the first place?

11

"I'm trying to locate a woman who worked here," I said to the pastor's secretary who stood before a magnetized announcement board in one corner of the church office. She peered into a box of plastic letters. "She played the organ and gave music lessons in town."

The secretary looked back up at the magnet board. "Not the organist anymore." She knocked out 'Fishers of Men, Potluck,' with a single swipe.

"Do you know where she is?"

The woman scrabbled in a box for more letters.

"Convalescent home."

"Is she ill?"

"Wouldn't know."

"Can you tell me where the home is?" Silence. The woman peered at the letters as though seeing the answer. Finally, "Two blocks east."

"Do you know her?"

"Used to."

"What's her name?"

"Twilah," the woman answered grudgingly. "Twilah Chan. Reynolds before that."

"Does she still give piano lessons?"

"Wouldn't know." I watched as she applied a message across the board: 'Lift up your voice.' "Doubt it."

I reached into her box of letters and affixed a message of my own: "Thanx." She watched me gravely until the telephone rang.

"First United Methodist Church, good morning, God bless you, remember that today is the first day of the rest of your life, Rhetta Mae Jackson speaking, how may I help you?"

12

THE DIRECTOR OF THE CONVALESCENT HOME gave me Twilah Chan's address, a once-fine three-story home now converted into apartments. With its assortment of drapes, curtains, and shades, the old house looked antic and off-center. It sat on the wrong side of the street: odd-numbered on the even-numbered side.

"Chan, Apartment G," read one of the scratched, black mailboxes running along the back wall of the porch. No one answered the doorbell and I let myself into a shabby hall-sitting room with a worn carpet and an assortment of armchairs that all needed cleaning. Through an interior doorway I found Apartment A on the left, B on the right. I followed the narrow hall, feeling like an intruder. At the end, Apartment C took up the entire back part of the house.

I returned to the front hall and climbed a stairway with handsome but scratched finials and rubber foot treads curling at the edges. Upstairs I followed a dim passage straight ahead. Under a low-watt bulb burning in a ceiling socket, I knocked on Apartment G. Quick footsteps approached from the inside rooms. Probably a caretaker or home health aide, I thought. The door opened and a vigorous-looking white-haired woman, tall in spite of a slight stoop, smiled down at me.

"Mrs. Chan?"

"Yes, indeed."

Over her shoulder I glimpsed a room with white walls and colorful paintings creating a vivid blur. Her hair was cut short, and her face was bony and austere, with a long nose, straight and narrow, and full but unsensual mouth. Black eyes snapped down at me.

"My name is Virginia Johnstone," I said.

"How nice to meet you, Virginia." She opened the door wider. "What can I do for you?" Beyond her, an Asian man sat at a desk facing two large windows. He turned around to acknowledge me with a reserved expression. Beside him a broad-leafed plant, very green in the half light of the gray day, rested on a stand.

"I understand you are a pianist."

She looked at me. Didn't just look at me. Her eyes pierced me. "Yes, I am."

"I'm a piano student," I said, "and I'll be staying in Hilliard for a while. I'm looking for a teacher."

"When?"

I was puzzled.

"When do you want to start?" Until now I hadn't noticed she wore overalls. Bib overalls hooked over a plaid shirt. On her feet were hiking boots; on her ears were plain hoop earrings. A bracelet of Indian design, silver and turquoise, circled her wrist.

"I'd like to start as soon as possible."

"How about right now?"

The answer shocked me. I wanted to know her better and to avoid her. "Would you like to meet my husband?"

I advanced through the doorway.

"My husband, Arturo," she stated, stepping back so the two of us could see each other.

"How do you do, Mr. Chan."

"Arturo, please," he said with the trace of an accent and a gracious bow of the head. "Would you care to sit down?"

"Well, thank you. I came without calling first and I don't want to take your time."

"We have time," said Twilah. She slid her hands deep in her pockets. "Have you played the piano long?"

"Five years."

"I see," she said. "You're just getting to the interesting stages, then."

"Oh, I am."

She smiled. "Do you have a piano? Because"—she pulled one hand out of her pocket and gestured toward the bookcases, the green plant, Mr. Chan—"I don't, as you can see."

"Well, I have a piano which I think you've played," I said cautiously. "It's in the old hotel down on the water."

One brown-spotted hand went to her denim bib. "It's a terrible piano."

"It's terrible."

"Are you living there?"

"Well, yes, I am." I tightened my hold on the music roll. "Until I go back to Seattle. I'm from Seattle."

"How did you know I've played that piano?"

"Mr. Raithel at the music store told me. He sent me to the convalescent hospital, they sent me to the Methodist Church, and the secretary sent me here."

Arturo looked amused. "You've left a trail, Twilah."

Twilah Chan didn't seem amused. She squared her shoulders. "Anytime you're ready," she said.

"I walked over here. I can't offer you a ride."

"Let's walk, then."

I decided she was desperate for students. As soon as she'd gotten a parka from the closet and said good-bye to Arturo, we descended the stairs of the apartment house and left the drab entryway behind. The gray cloud cover had come apart, leaving a last few tatters to float in a blue sky. As we reached the sidewalk Twilah looked back at the house. Beside the green plant, Mr. Chan, lean and courtly, waved to us from the window.

"What are you working on now?" she asked, walking at a pace that forced me to keep up.

"I just bought Beethoven's early sonatas." I slowed my steps to pull out the music roll.

"The first one has a nice Trio. It's a beautiful, simple melody." We stopped in the middle of the sidewalk and I held the book while she pointed to the notes, humming as she indicated the underlying rhythm with her left hand.

"I'm learning a Chopin etude, and I play several pieces in the Well-Tempered Klavier," I bragged after we had gone farther.

"Well, well," she said. "You have the right spirit." Looking sharply at an orange cat that dashed across our path, she added, "Have you lived in Hilliard long?"

"A week," I replied. With the change in weather and our brisk walk we were both growing warm. I pushed back my hood. She turned to scrutinize me with those bright black eyes. "Oh, my. You've hardly been here at all."

"I'm on a leave of absence from my job. I . . ." I faltered. "I needed to get away from the city for a while."

She asked no more questions and we walked the last block in silence. I inserted my steel key into the old lock and entered the building ahead of her. The building must have been quite different when she taught here. Clean and busy.

"Starfish!" she exclaimed as we began climbing the stairs. "Look at the beautiful stones and shells. Have you collected these?"

"No," I said, for the first time wishing I had. "I'm renting an apartment that belongs to someone else. She's the one who collected these specimens."

"Do you know her?"

I shook my head.

"The building draws lost souls," she said, "and then waits to see what happens to them."

"I'm not a lost soul," I said defensively. "And the woman who lives here is very creative."

I unlocked the door to my kitchen. Twilah sniffed.

"Do you know her?"

"Slightly. Everyone in Hilliard knows something about everyone else." She was looking around the room as if assessing damage. "I believe this is where the hotel manager lived." She walked to the window and looked down at the channel. "For a desperate period of about six weeks I actually lived in the room where I taught."

I opened my mouth to ask why, but she gave me a disarming smile and said conversationally, "No one knew. Except Arturo, of course." She sent me an arch glance and began telling me what she expected of her piano students. "Work. Yes, of course: work. Self-discipline. You may think that's the most important thing. It isn't. The important thing is the wish to learn, to grow. Unreasonable devotion. Without it, one can't stick with the work. Or if one sticks with it, the work becomes a mere habit."

"I don't like to live by habit."

"Of course not. Furthermore . . ." I listened through her fluctuations: reflective, critical, aloof, sympathetic. She began to remove her parka.

"You may want to leave that on until I get the music room warmed up," I suggested. "In the meantime I'll put on the kettle."

Still wearing coats, we carried our teacups down the cold, dirty hall. I turned on the electric heater and left the room. When I returned with a second chair she was looking out over the street. "Nothing much changes in the old hotel. Except the people, of course. We come and go."

"When were you here?"

"Thirty years ago."

"What was the hotel like then? What did the room look like?"

She set down her cup and took one of the straight chairs. "There were a number of permanent renters and a few guests each night, usually going to the islands or coming back from the islands. They used to tromp in after the seven o'clock ferry."

"Was the room furnished?"

"Not very." She played several chords and shuddered. "Same piano. It sounded a little less tinny with a rug and curtains. I put up wall hangings. They softened the tone somewhat." She set her cup on top of the piano and took off her parka. "Enough talk," she said. "Let's get to work."

I opened Bach. Playing for her was different than playing for my Seattle teacher. He stopped me often and if, in the midst of a grueling lesson, I occasionally reached a state where music seemed to come from deep within, he was sure to tap the keys with a pointer and break the spell. Now I was playing better than ever on a rinky-tink piano and without much practice at that. I finished and sat with my hands in my lap, not looking anywhere.

Finally she said, "You play beautifully. It will be a pleasure to teach you."

The bare music room with Twilah in it opened and expanded. It was as if she stood at the gate of some new world, welcoming me. We went through the fugue, working out themes. I heard, really heard, all the voices at the same time. For years I'd been dutifully bringing out first one, then its echo, left hand, right hand, outside voice, inside voice. But this was the first time I heard them all simultaneously, each in its perfect relation to the whole. Bach warmed me; Twilah warmed me; the sun warmed me. I thought I might never need the electric heater again.

13

I begged Ron to let the children come to Hilliard for a weekend.

"I'll pick them up and bring them back to Seattle," I promised.

Finally he offered to drive them himself, but only because he was planning to go on to Orcas Island by ferry. The next morning I watched for them at the bedroom window, eager to show them the boatyard, the docks, the beach. They climbed the stairs to meet me, walked quickly through my rooms, and stopped at the bedroom window where they scanned the boatyard across the street in a quick, aloof glance. They put their sleeping bags on the old sofa and asked where the TV was.

"No television," I said. "I don't have one." They struggled to digest the information.

"Want to look around the hotel?" I asked. They didn't. "Or see the docks? There are a lot of interesting boats tied up."

Lawrence studied the ceiling, the dingy cornice, the cracks in the plaster showing through yellowed wallpaper. "This place is old," he said.

"And dirty," added Matt.

"The hallways and empty rooms, yes. But my rooms aren't dirty," I said. "Well, not very dirty, anyway."

The boys went over to the sofa and perched on their rolled-up sleeping bags as if, when they flew from this place, they would at least take off from something familiar.

"Why do you want to live in an old building like this?" Matt asked.

"It's cheap," I said, sitting beside them. "I'm living off of savings. And—well, it sort of intrigues me." Silence. I tried again. "It's a short-term experiment. I'm trying to learn a lot of things fast."

"Dad doesn't like this place, either," said Lawrence.

"I understand your viewpoint and his," I said. Once again, the wall. The three of them, Ron and Matthew and Lawrence, arrayed and fortified against someone. Someone they could not trust or understand.

"But why?" Lawrence demanded. "There's lots of old buildings in Seattle you can live in." He cocked his head and listened hard for an answer that made sense to him. He seemed younger than he'd been even two weeks earlier. Much too young to be without me.

"You misunderstand," I said. But behind that misunderstanding was something he truly understood and couldn't say: *Why have you left us again?* I wished I could promise to come back to the city immediately. More than come back to the city, to come back home, back to the neighborhood, back to the children. For a moment I imagined that I could, indeed, battle the demon inside me that longed to be away from Ron's small circle, away from the University dinner parties and discreet comparisons of academic rank, IQ, possessions; for a moment I wanted to hold on for the next nine years until the children were through school.

Matt sat quietly, waiting for an answer, dispute already in his serious eyes.

"I'm missing a great deal by not living with you," I said, surprised by my tears. "Other mothers see their children grow day by day. I wanted to stay at home with you boys and have Daddy move out," I said, "but he wouldn't agree. And I didn't think I had the right to take away his children."

"We're *your* children, too," Matt said in a sullen tone. I nodded violently. I'd gone on my knees on the cushion. I was at Lawrence's feet, lower than he, since he sat high on the sleeping roll in a corner of the sofa. I was actually cradling one of his feet. I feared this emotion; I was terrified it would hurt the boys and me.

Lawrence began to cry softly. The sullenness in Matt's eyes drained away, and now the three of us were crying together. I made a bigger space for myself between the sleeping bags and pushed backwards into the upholstery. Buried in the warm hollow, I reached up to hug one boy, then the other, my head in their ribs, my nose running.

Matthew rubbed his eyes and looked down at me. "Can't you at least live somewhere better than here?"

"Which do you hate most?" I asked. "Hilliard or the old hotel?"

Lawrence's face was rumpled and streaked. "Both." He scooted lower and laid his head on top of mine. Matt wiped his nose on his sleeve and moved in close. After a while, instead of shock and fright and guilt, I began to feel warm, almost cozy, sunk deep in the broken-down couch. On my left, Lawrence made a protective roof. On my right, Matt's body was heavy and warm. I pulled my arms down from where they were going numb around the kids' necks.

"Please give me three months in Hilliard," I said quietly. The three of us sat without speaking. After a while they got down off the sleeping bags and said if there wasn't a TV in the house, we might as well go see the docks.

They were not impressed.

The next night, Saturday, I took them to Hilliard's only theater. But the movie was too adult for them and too childish for me. On the way home I pulled more than my weight of the conversation.

"Want to make some popcorn?" I asked, driving down nearly-abandoned High Street.

"No. Let's go someplace for ice cream."

"I don't think there's anything open this late. Just the tavern."

"It's only eight-thirty, Mom."

"Yes, but remember, this is Hilliard."

Silence, and then the repeated question: "How can you live here?"

"I have a piano teacher," I said. "I'm learning more than I thought I could."

"You have a piano teacher in Seattle," Matt said.

"Yeah," said Lawrence.

"Ah, but not as fine a teacher as I have in Hilliard. Let me tell you how I found her," and I embarked on the story of my search. I may have dramatized Mr. Raithel and his secondhand music store somewhat. I'm sure I imbued the convalescent home and church with more mystery and intrigue than they possessed. Twilah required no embellishment. When I stopped talking Lawrence said,

"What time is Dad coming back?"

Ron picked them up Sunday afternoon. "As long as you've come this far," he advised me, "you ought to go on over to Orcas. What a beautiful island." He glanced at the woodburner and crooked kitchen cabinets. "Why did you choose Hilliard?"

"I like Hilliard. It's quiet."

"Yeah, it is, Dad," said Matt, rolling his eyes. All three of them looked up at the high, smoky ceiling.

"Well, bye," said Lawrence as they all moved to the door.

"Is there any way I can bribe you up here again?" I felt like breaking down. They smiled weakly at my weak joke. Their dad was already halfway down among the starfish. They followed.

"See you in Seattle," I managed.

Lawrence looked up at me where I stood at the top of the stairs. "Where will you stay?"

"I'll find someplace. A friend's. Or I might just come down for the day and drive back. You're only an hour away."

"Soccer on Saturday," said Matt.

"What time?"

"Ten in the morning," Ron said. His reddish blond hair was thinning at the crown. From the top of the stairs I saw more than his balding head. I looked down through the years at the slender young man I'd loved, so quick in movement, so smart that he'd had five graduate fellowships to choose from. I'd been afraid he would meet someone else in graduate school, but he never stopped coming to see me in my college a few miles away. We couldn't wait to get married. I left school after two years. Ron climbed the academic ranks quickly, we had the boys, we bought the house, and then—was that all? Was that it? Was that to be my life? Years of dull adulthood spent getting the children through high school and college, then adjusting to their marriages and children, then retirement, and death?

Going to court reporting school had helped. Working helped, too, for a while. But my boredom had only gone underground. It always came up for light and air when things were nearly perfect. And things were almost always nearly perfect.

Ron held the door open for the kids, gave one last critical glance up the stairwell, and then they were gone. My wish to start the visit over again, to properly explain to all three of them what I was doing here, to show them Hilliard in such a way that the boys would want to come back, was so intense it left me weak-kneed. I locked the door to the street. Slowly proceeding upstairs, rearranging specimens as I went, letting tears fall on starfish, sand dollars, clam shells, I climbed to my rooms and sat on the bed to watch the shipbuilders work. The buzz and snap of the arc welder did not quite cover the sound of my family pulling away from the curb.

14

I TRIED TO READ, to nap, but ended up walking aimlessly through the rooms of the apartment. Finally I changed into clean slacks and a long-sleeved burgundy sweater. Twilah had invited me for a light supper that evening. "Arturo is used to eating a big meal in the middle of the day and a snack in the evening," she'd said. "Tea, he calls it. He lived in England for a time."

When? I wanted to ask. Why? How did you meet? But Twilah didn't invite questions and I didn't ask.

I knocked on the door to Apartment G and Arturo opened it. Someone else was in the room, a lean man with a weathered face and quiet manner.

"Mrs. Johnstone," said Mr. Chan, "meet Twilah's son, Gregory Reynolds." Gregory's hand, when he shook mine, was cool and calloused.

"Virginia!" Twilah said, sweeping in with a plate of cold cuts and cheese. "You've met?" She was busy scanning her son's Levis and work boots. "You might have worn something with a bit more—gloss."

"I just dropped by," he said without much interest. "I didn't know you were having high tea." His mother gave a superior look, pushed hard on the swinging door, and disappeared into the kitchen. I took the chair Mr. Chan offered. He had so much exotic dignity that I found it hard to say "Arturo."

"Please call me by my first name," he urged.

"If you'll call me Virginia."

Gregory sat down at one end of the sofa. The three of us talked, interrupted now and then by Twilah bringing in sandwiches and salad to the sideboard behind us. If her son had not dressed with enough gloss, she had more than made up for it with her dramatic floor-length skirt fashioned from a bright patchwork of felts, corduroys and velvets. Her blouse was stark white, hand-embroidered in white thread by a patient native worker somewhere in a poorer part of the world.

The light outside had faded without warning. Folk art from somewhere in Central or South America—fabrics, wood carvings, drawings—brightened the white walls and plain furniture. Arturo's fine oriental face glowed copper, and his immaculate hair shone like black lacquer. In the background, adding another layer of folklore to the room, a cd played Moussorgski's *Pictures at an Exhibition*: Mother Russia, her people's music, oxen plodding through the steppe.

"Are you working on a publication?" I asked Arturo, nodding in the direction of his desk, which was covered with books and writing paper.

"I'm working on an article at the present time," he replied. Not wanting to burble—'Really? How wonderful, how exciting,' et cetera—I waited, hoping he would explain further. He didn't.

"What is the subject of your article?" And where, I wanted to ask, did you get your name, 'Arturo'?

"Implications of Monetary Systems in Twentieth-Century Revolutions of Central America."

"That sounds like a very complex subject."

"It is part of a larger work."

"Arturo lived in Costa Rica for a number of years," said Gregory.

"Hilliard is a long way from Costa Rica," I said.

"A very long way. Farther than I ever expected to come."

"He was born in China and moved with his family to Costa Rica in – what year was it, Arturo?"

"1935."

"The Chinese Revolution?" I surprised myself by remembering.

"I was fifteen. My father feared Japan and he feared the civil war in China. So he brought his family to Costa Rica where one of my great-uncles had lived for many years."

"He was not Communist, then?"

"No. In those days the communists were poor peasants. You've heard of the Long March? We were in Shanghai, far from the rural poor. My father had been educated in England. Oxford. Christ Church. His father was a Christian convert. We were all Presbyterians."

"I see," I said, without seeing.

"You've heard of the opium trade?"

"Then or now?" Gregory said. Twilah made another trip through the swinging door.

"There is nothing new about drug traffic," Arturo said, arch and amused, before continuing. "As a young man I gave most of my money away. I felt I had missed the revolution, which indeed I had, but at least I would not be among the greedy of the earth."

Gregory leaned his head against the sofa back as if, having drawn Arturo into conversation, he could now leave the social activity to others.

"I was too early for the revolution in China and too late for the revolution in Central America. So close to the important developments of the twentieth century, yet never part of them."

"But you write about them?"

"It is my destiny to be an onlooker."

Gregory remained silent. Against the Indian blanket hanging on the wall behind him, his head seemed well shaped, and his hair showed dark and curly. I looked around for Twilah but she'd returned to the kitchen.

"Why do you feel so strongly about revolution?" I asked, wondering if Arturo was a communist, ashamed of myself for not knowing exactly what a communist was, what a revolutionary was, nor even if they were the same thing anymore.

"Detaching oneself from colonial powers and ruling classes is at the heart of the twentieth century," he said with quiet intensity. "It is the effort not to be dominated, not to have ourselves stolen."

"But you're living in a rich and powerful country," I said before I thought. "That is . . ." I tried to withdraw the implication that he was now among the dominant. But Arturo held up his hand, forbidding the social lie.

"Only these last few years have I begun to realize what I am doing. It is difficult to overcome the love of comfort. It is the true prison of the mind."

I thought: I gave up comfort in Seattle and came to Hilliard.

"It is easy," he continued, "to comply with the rich and powerful when offered a poor guarantee of safety and a paltry portion of the spoils. Revolutionary movements can be likened to the individual separating from the all-powerful parent. My books . . . what I am pursuing is an idea that interests me deeply. Colonialism, patriarchy, must be outgrown."

"Matriarchy," said Greg. The door swung open, then shut, as the matriarch disappeared into the kitchen.

"Individuality must be struggled for, endlessly," Arturo said. Slowly he reached into his back pocket and took out a white handkerchief. "That is something we Chinese are not very good at." He wiped his mouth as if to erase the trait. "Nor has independence of thought been sufficiently achieved in Central America."

"It probably hasn't been sufficiently achieved anywhere," I murmured, wishing to sound intelligent.

"The Central Americans have a saying," he said, returning the handkerchief to his pocket. "'*Obedezco pero no cumplo*. I obey but do not comply.' It is the colonized's substitute for separation."

"Insidious," said Greg.

"It is, indeed," said Arturo. "Although it permits the dominated to live, it promotes weakness."

Twilah burst into the room carrying three stacked plates.

"May I help?" I asked.

"You can help by helping yourself," she said, and indicated I was to come to the buffet. I stood, and Arturo and Gregory followed There was little talk except Twilah now and then exclaiming she'd forgotten this or that as she strode into the kitchen. The three of us filled our plates and sat down again.

"Well," said Twilah, coming to a standstill beside Arturo, "I have a toast."

"Then I'd better pour the wine," Gregory said wryly. Arturo pulled up a chair for his wife while Gregory filled our glasses with red wine. When he'd seated himself, we each held up our glass, the wine bringing out even more the pristine whiteness of the walls, the bright touches in the room. With full darkness enclosing the fine old house, Twilah turned toward me.

"To Virginia, woman, pianist, life traveler."

They lifted their glasses seriously. I had already lifted mine, having no idea I would be drinking to me. Twilah seemed to know me better than I knew myself. Not wanting to be separated from her musical and personal authority, I felt accepted in this small room and happier than I had been in a long time.

15

PIANO LESSONS AND HOURS OF PRACTICE consumed me that first month in Hilliard. Twilah guided me. Going beyond pleasure, beyond my own personality, was far from easy: sometimes I left the music room in tears; sometimes I wanted to scream at my fingers, at the piano, at my inadequate musicianship; at the music itself, pushing to get out. After these intense sessions I would sit in the bedroom staring across at the ship. It was such an enormous vessel that I doubted the hull would be finished by the time I had to leave.

Not only did Twilah lead me through the labyrinths of music, but she got me an unlikely job which I came to think of as 'The Christmas Gig.' It started with a pounding on the beveled glass door at street level.

"Hello! Anybody home?"

I jumped up from the edge of my bed where I had been watching the shipyard. No one ever came here except Twilah, and that was on Tuesdays and Fridays: today was Thursday.

"Coming!" I yelled, sidestepping the specimens.

"Are you Virginia Johnstone?" asked a poised woman with a jingling charm bracelet as I opened the door. I took an immediate dislike to her. Heather Desmond had just been to the hairdresser and the scent of beauty care products preceded her. Delicate nose, sculptured cheeks, slim wrists and ankles were beautiful bones exposed outside of her swirling cashmere coat. Two children in private school skirt, slacks, and coats stood beside her. How fortunate she was to have them near.

"Yes, I'm Virginia."

"We're friends of Twilah Chan. I'm Heather Desmond and these are my children, Leslie and Kevin."

"How do you do."

She touched her hair and the bracelet jingled. "Twilah says you are a wonderful pianist."

"Twilah is my teacher," I said, and left it at that.

"We're having a Christmas party on the 10th of December and wondered if you'd be interested in playing for us. Some Christmas music, carols, some nice background sounds."

Was Twilah referring a job to me? She hadn't mentioned it.

"Well, let me think about it. I've never played at a party before."

"I'm sure it would be easy for you. Just some nice background music and carols." She glanced up the stairs. "How's twenty-five dollars?"

Somebody paying me to entertain. It was a novel idea. A job in Hilliard.

"Did you ask Twilah to play?"

"She doesn't play in public anymore," said Heather, touching her hair again as she looked in the glass of the half-open door. "Besides," she added, "Twilah and Arturo are invited guests."

"Santa Claus will be there with lots of toys and things," said the little girl.

"I'm getting one hundred video games," said the boy. His sister looked at him with pity and disdain.

All at once Christmas began to bear down on me, and the fact that loomed largest about the holiday season was my sons' absence. Or more accurately, mine.

"My husband is the administrator of the hospital," Heather said, as if offering a reference.

"Executive director," added the girl.

"We enjoy entertaining and we like to do something a little special at our parties."

"I'm not an experienced performer."

"Oh, we don't want a performance."

"Background music," said the girl.

"All right," I said. "Do you have anything special you'd like?"

"I'll make up a list of some tunes and mail them to you." Heather drew back her head and looked at the hotel above us. "What is your mailing address?"

"I—I'm not sure," I admitted. There was a faint number at the bottom of the rusted mailbox. "217."

Heather looked embarrassed for me. She glanced up High Street, perhaps unable to believe it was still High Street here at the lower end of town. With a short, jeweled pen she jotted down the address in a little notebook.

"Thank you, Virginia," she said. "We'll look forward to it. December 10th."

I climbed back up my stairs, rearranging the specimens as I went. I was surprised Twilah had given this Heather Desmond my name. Still, it would be a chance to see more of Hilliard. And after all, it was my first paying job as a musician.

The Christmas lights that began appearing in town made me sad. I bought my sons' gifts early, wrapped them, and put them in the middle room where I intended to set up a tree. Talking to them on the phone was satisfying in a small way. Relieved, I think, at not having to come to the end of the world to visit their mom, they were voluble and informative, yet ready to hang up much sooner than I. Soccer, school, neighbor kids, their dad's requirements, they sounded busy and happy. Ron was doing a good job with them. I arranged to spend time in Seattle during their holiday vacation.

16

THROUGH FLOOR-TO-CEILING GLASS I saw the baby grand piano, its lid braced open at the half-way position. Potted jades and decorated star pines flanked the front door where I stood ringing the bell. Moonlight and starlight fell through lathe work above me and landed in slats on the cement and aggregate below. Through the glass I watched well-dressed men and women laugh and drink and eat.

"Virginia!" Heather flung open the door and grasped my hand with both of hers, demonstrating practiced affection. She was beautiful in a floor-length hostess gown, pure white. "*Les enfants* are eager to meet you!"

This surprised me somewhat, but I understood when she led me down the hall and into the family room where the children were kept, evidently waiting for the nice lady who was going to play the piano.

"We'll be ready for music in about half an hour," said Heather. "Make yourself comfortable." She kissed her daughter on the top of her blonde head, patted her son, waved to the other seven or eight children, and was gone.

They immediately began overtures to the new lady whose status was quite clear: hired help who happened to play the piano.

"Do you know how to play 'I'm a Little Holly Berry?'" asked a blue-eyed angel of a child who, unreasonably, angered me. Her status was clear: a beautiful, cooperative little girl who, unlike myself, would grow up to have a happy, conventional life in which she did nothing unsafe or unexpected. Her parents, whom I didn't even know, angered me, too. They were not separated from their child at Christmas. I swallowed my temper and, house musician that I was, encouraged them in a little dress rehearsal. They sang with enthusiasm. Finally I told the children I needed to go to the bathroom and one of the girls showed me where it was. When I returned, Heather was waiting.

"Come and meet my husband," she commanded over one shoulder. We all followed her along the hallway.

"Morgan!" she exclaimed to a slender man in a dark suit and a silk shirt left open two buttons' worth. His hair was permed and sprayed into a wary configuration. A gold chain glinted at his throat. "Morgan, this is Virginia . . ."

"Johnstone," I said, looking the man in the eye.

"Virginia." He squeezed my hand. "Wonderful of you to come."

"Not at all," I said truthfully. The guests stopped talking for a moment as Heather arranged the children in front of the candelabra.

"Daddy! Daddy!" cried one of the little boys dressed in a miniature jacket, tie, and creased slacks that had to be cleaned rather than laundered. His father rushed over and mollified him with an hors d'oeuvre. I made my way to the piano and sat down, first opening a Christmas songbook I'd purchased at Mr. Raithel's shop a few days before.

The children sang their hearts out. When 'Jingle Bells' had taken its final beating, the children were paraded out by a dark woman in a white uniform. I began to play something soft, what I hoped would be a nice transition to cocktail party music later. But 'I'm Dreaming of a White Christmas' was not heard by anyone. Artificial candles on an enormous fir tree winked just beyond the piano. Realtor talk from a man who was developing an island as fast as a wallet can be whipped out of a back pocket rose and fell in aggressive thrusts. Furiously on the make, he stood near my left elbow for the final phase of his sales pitch.

"You'd be in on the ground floor," he assured someone. "The lots are falling like dominoes."

"How's the water out there?" asked the prospect. "They drilled a well yet?"

"Testing laboratory says there's no problem, no problem." The realtor glowed above his drink, deeply convinced.

"What about State approval?"

"It's coming. It's coming. By the way, have you met" . . .and he introduced a man with a jaw so clean-shaven and taut that it gleamed. "Stephan is the lawyer for the development . . ." Words like 'tract', 'homeowners association', 'financing package' mingled with my arrangement of 'Oh Little Town of Bethlehem'. A county commissioner, according to the lawyer, was expected at the party and he promised an introduction. As they walked off, the realtor bent down and breathed into my ear, "That's pretty, honey." His cigarette smoke lingered after he had gone.

On my right a woman with a lilting voice emitted an endless flow of wisdom. "He's still in denial . . . working it through . . . co-dependency . . . dysfunctional family . . ."

Aren't we all? I thought. I played lightly, hoping to get attention by not asking for it. But the ploy didn't work. I changed to something more aggressive, 'Oh Holy Night', which had a particularly loud climax. But Heather came over to the piano and suggested something quieter.

After a final run-through of 'Ave Maria', I was ready for a break. I'd played my set. I pushed back the piano bench, trying to think of a way to advance on the buffet without seeming presumptuous or, worse, hungry.

I took an experimental step in the direction of a seafood platter. Crackers surrounded a crab mixture molded to a salmon's shape. Heather caught me.

"You finished already?" she asked.

"Finished the set," I said professionally.

"Set?" she said. "Virginia, this is not a bar."

"Well, Heather," I said, though we were not on a first-name basis, "I'm on a break." With me, her house musician, she vacillated between chummy and aloof, no more sure, I began to suspect, of her status than I was of mine. We both wanted recognition and were pretty sure we hadn't done anything to deserve it.

Heather's husband, the hospital administrator, seemed to skate across the rug toward us. "And how are the beautiful ladies?" he asked, well-oiled. Heather stiffened a little, perhaps at being lumped into the same compliment with the entertainment. "Finished your set?" asked Morgan Desmond. I smiled and nodded.

"What do you do for a living, Virginia?" he asked. I considered lying. Professional musician visiting a friend in Hilliard, charming little town, how amusing, here to rest up between tours, blah-blah-blah.

"I'm a court reporter," I said.

He beamed. "Ah. The little black box. And do you work at the courthouse?"

"Not at the courthouse," I answered. He'd forgotten the question. "I'm a freelance deposition reporter. In Seattle."

His eyes slipped back to mine, briefly roused to interest again. "We have several lawyers here tonight, Virginia. And, of course, doctors from the hospital staff."

Heather laid a hand on her husband's arm. "Virginia needs to get back to the piano," she reminded him. As if to fortify her position, she whispered something in her husband's ear. Good-naturedly he pulled out his wallet and withdrew two tens and a five.

"Not here," his wife said irritably. But he was already thanking me and handing me money. I accepted it with a perfectly easy gesture, refusing to dignify the exchange by mincing etiquette. Heather's gaze, silver, blue, emphasized by a single velvet line drawn beneath each almond-shaped eye, was riveted on the bills.

She was afraid of being tacky. And afraid no one would notice she wasn't tacky. I stood holding the money, even changed hands and kept it clearly in view for anyone to see while I strung out my chat with Morgan.

"Here comes one of my doctors," he announced. I folded the bills conspicuously and put them in my pocket, like a barmaid dropping a tip into her apron, and turned toward the piano. But I stopped abruptly. Standing in the center of the room, tall, elegant, distinguished, was my piano teacher. Mr. Chan—Arturo—hovered in the background. Twilah's craggy face was made up for society: powder, lipstick, eye-liner. She approached Morgan and laid one of her large, strong hands on his arm, transferred it back to her drink, then repeated the sequence over again. The hand followed a rhythm; touch, press, move. I thought she was pretending not to see me.

I'd been wrong to crack open my flat but satisfactory life in Seattle. Watching her, I knew I didn't belong in Hilliard.

In the middle of 'It's Beginning to Look a Lot Like Christmas' my superior amusement at the airs of the Desmonds and their guests faltered. My stagey, sarcastic state of mind slipped and despair over the divorce lifted to reveal a deeper despair. The rooms in the old hotel aren't mine. I'm just staying here till the real tenant, the absent woman, gets back. My home is in Seattle. My home is somewhere else.

17

I WAS AT EYE LEVEL with the broken downspout on the back wing of the old hotel. It had been raining all morning, and water ran along the gutter under the eaves and emptied in a noisy stream. Later, the pipe would resume its steady, musical drip. The mud underneath never quite dried between rains. I sat in the kitchen, drinking tea, watching the rain and listening.

The telephone rang. It was Gregory, Twilah's son.

"How are you getting along in Hilliard by now?" It felt good to be talking to a man; his voice was deep and down-to-earth.

"Fine. It's quiet."

"Would you like some company?" he asked. "Would you like to have dinner?"

The wind took the water from the downspout and bent its stream.

"Nothing fancy," he added.

"Conversation over dinner might be nice for a change." I wasn't interested in dating. Jerry had been my last and final date. "Let's meet somewhere."

"Okay. We can meet somewhere." There was a silence. "Playing the piano a lot, are you?"

"Every day. Two lessons a week and lots of practice."

"Well, how would Friday be?"

"Friday would be fine."

"The Cabbage Patch. Best food around. It's across the channel from the reservation. You take Fishery Road to the reservation cut-off." He paused. "Are you sure you don't want me to pick you up?"

"Thanks, but I'll find it. Six-thirty?"

"Fine."

Piano lessons. A gig at a Christmas party. Now dinner for two. Life in Hilliard was not as quiet as I'd expected it to be. Contrary to city opinion, the town was not quite the end of the world.

But it seemed like the Cabbage Patch was. In the dark, one country road looks pretty much like another. It took me a while to find the intersection where I'd made a wrong turn. I crossed a rickety bridge and sensed rather than saw a canal or some kind of slough running alongside the road. I knew the Indians fished near here. Finally I spotted the sign I'd been looking for, inconspicuous and almost outside my headlights: 'Cabbage Patch.' I parked on gravel and entered a two-story farmhouse with a wide porch running along the front. What must have been the old double parlor and dining room had been converted into a restaurant.

Except for a party of two at a table across the room, Gregory was the only diner: he looked introspective, even moody. I slid onto the chair opposite him and ordered a glass of wine to go with his ale. The way he held his head, back a little, looking at me through the lower part of his smoky gray eyes, reminded me of how he'd leaned back against his mother's sofa the day I'd met him.

"Sorry I'm late."

"Hard to find, isn't it?" There was a sly, *I-told-you-so* intent in the comment. The fire in the potbellied stove flared, then resumed its murmur.

"The heat feels good," I said, flexing my back and moving nearer the stove. It had been silly to insist on driving alone. Such a dark, wet night.

"I don't know why I insisted on driving myself," I said. "I've been pretty solitary up here."

"Hilliard will do that to you," said Greg. "The weather and the Sound can cut you off."

"How long have you lived here?"

"I was raised here, left, and came back. And sometimes I wonder about the 'came back' part."

"You're sorry to be in Hilliard?"

"Nah," he said without drama. In the silence a glob of pitch exploded in the stove. "My mom says you found a piano in the old hotel."

"Mr. Raithel told me about it. He's the one who told me about your mom, too. If he hadn't, I'd probably still be driving to Seattle for lessons and getting nowhere."

"But here you're getting somewhere?"

"Yes, I am. I don't know where, exactly," I admitted, "but I'm learning more than I ever thought I could." I told him about reading the ad and coming up to Hilliard almost on a whim.

"I read the ads all the time," he said. "You can usually find a hell of a deal, whether you need it or not."

"My place came furnished," I said, laying a sardine on a cracker. "Such as it is."

"Why did you choose the old hotel?"

"The price was right," I said, "and I have a view of the water. And, of course, the red curtains."

"Red curtains?"

I nodded. "At the front and back windows. There's a studio, too, full of paintings and drawings and needlework and . . . lots of stuff. Whoever lived in those rooms is a talented person."

There was a subtle change in Greg's expression, as if a layer had been peeled back.

"Did you know her?" I asked. "Marguerite something-or-other?"

He slid his mug from one hand to the other, shuffleboard-style, along the table.

"Everybody knows everybody else in this town," he said.

"She's coming back," I informed him. "At least the landlord says she's coming back."

"I doubt it."

"Why?"

He shrugged. "Why come back to the end of the world?"

"I think of it as the *edge* of the world. The continent lies east."

"The leading edge," he said ironically, and drank some ale.

"I wonder why she came in the first place," I said. "Or did she grow up here? Oh, wait. The landlord said she's from Kansas."

He nodded. I wondered if he knew her. I wondered if his end-of-the-world fatalism was a general opinion or related to the absent woman. Or to himself.

"Was she hiding from something?"

He gave me a direct look accompanied by an indirect silence. *Aren't we all hiding from something?* he seemed to be saying.

"Yes, perhaps we are," I answered. This wordless communication, both pleasing and worrisome, surprised me. I didn't need smoky gray eyes and curly hair here in Hilliard.

"How long are you planning to stay?"

"A couple of months," I said. "I'll be out of money by then"

"That's the tricky part. What do you do for a living?"

I told him about deposition reporting, the ups and downs of freelancing. I looked around for a menu. "Do we order or what?"

"Jim cooks one main dish a day. Whatever he fixes, that's what we eat."

I watched Jim, an American Indian, serve the other table and return to the kitchen.

"What do you do for a living?"

He pulled a folded piece of paper from the pocket of his flannel shirt and spread it out between us. "Just got this today." It was the announcement of a workshop for blacksmiths. His name was listed on the cover as a demonstrator. "I'm just one of several," he said. "Two are coming up from Oregon. The main guy is the blacksmith at Williamsburg, Virginia. It was a coup getting him."

"I'm impressed." I studied Greg's face. A strong nose like his mother's, but gray-to-hazel eyes very unlike hers. They were soft and set deep under a weathered forehead. His hair was dark and seriously curly; he obviously paid no attention to it.

He put down the mug of ale and pointed out the topic to be covered in the workshop: Damascus steel. His hands, when he carefully refolded the brochure, were as I remembered, large, calloused, with big knuckles and long, tapering fingers. His body, too, tapered from muscular shoulders down toward the narrow crown of pelvis, the bony hub of the body. He returned the brochure to his pocket.

"I'm all wrapped up in blacksmithing," he said with a self-conscious smile.

I smiled back. "It's wonderful to feel passionate about something."

Just then Jim came out of the kitchen bearing two thick plates of red snapper cooked in butter and garlic. Out of the corner of his eye he watched us eat, beating us to more salad, bread, lemon before we could ask. If he was surprised at the end of the meal, watching through the cook's window, to see us split the bill and divvy up the tip, his expression didn't show it.

"That man knows how to run a restaurant," I said to Greg as we walked through the fog to our cars. "His food is too good to have just a smidgin."

"Do you like ling cod?"

"You bet," I replied, feeling local.

"I'll have to see what I can do." We reached my car. Against the light from the restaurant window, Greg's profile was well-modeled, his throat and neck strong. Mist beaded his hair.

I inserted my key into the driver's door. "Do you fish commercially?"

"I quit four years ago." His eyes glanced from the car to me. "I still get all the fresh fish I want."

"You'd rather be blacksmithing."

"I'd rather be blacksmithing."

"I really didn't know there were still blacksmiths," I said, my hand on the door handle.

"There are a few of us around. In fact, the trade is growing. People like handmade work."

"Do you sell a lot of your stuff?"

"More and more all the time. Not enough to live on, though. I teach welding and something called fire arts at the community college."

I turned to face him.

"It's a name I dreamed up," he admitted.

"I'd like to see your work sometime."

He smiled without commitment. He opened my door and I got in.

"Want to meet me somewhere for a drink?" he asked.

"I'd better get home."

"The piano."

"I enjoyed dinner with you," I said. He closed the door, but stayed where he was, so I rolled down the window.

"My mom said she saw you the other evening at a party. Said you did a good job with the music."

"She recommended me. My first job as a musician," I said. "Not that anyone actually heard me."

"Mom heard you," he said.

I snapped on my headlights. "She barely said hello."

He jammed his hands into the pockets of his windbreaker and chopped at the gravel underfoot with one heel. "Well, she gets excited when she's around royalty." He looked idly into the fog. Then he smiled, turned his coat collar against the damp, and walked away. When he reached the bed of his pickup, he looked back and waved. I waved and shifted into reverse. Mist swirled in my headlights. His truck started up. With both sets of windshield wipers laboring, we pulled out of the gravel and left the Cabbage Patch to the wet night.

18

As weeks went by I needed less and less sleep and, in spite of the cold, I often awoke at five or six in the morning. then, wrapped in a robe and blanket, I would sit in the middle room where the baseboard heaters managed to push slightly warmed air a few inches off the floor.

One such morning, trailing a blanket from bed, I walked into the absent woman's studio, stopped under the light bulb, and pulled the string. Light struck the piñata, the mermaid, the miniature ceramic elephants swaying across the window sill. I blinked. It was a remarkable display. Such an outpour of feeling. So much *stuff*.

I spotted what looked like a booklet of poems, or perhaps a story, lying next to a pair of knitting needles, and I bent to pick it up.

'Superior Court of the State of Washington, County of Oakley' the transcript read. 'Twilah Chan, et ux, Plaintiffs, versus Fairhaven Convalescent Home and Marguerite Cleary, Defendants.' There was a case number. Centered on each page were the words: 'Deposition of Twilah Chan.' The blanket slid off my shoulders. I drew it back over myself and squatted on the floor. Marguerite Cleary. She'd scrawled it in books. She was the absent woman, the woman Greg doubted would come back, the woman whose studio I hardly ever entered.

Her name on the page awoke a series of nerves: I perceived her, not in my imagination, but in a cascade of comprehension traveling through my brain and down my spine. She was like a blood relation I'd heard about and was now going to meet.

As I fiddled with pages, snapping the transparent cover with my thumbnail, I knew she was real and I was afraid of her. I began reading and didn't look up again until the seven-o'clock whistle blew for the first shift in the boatyard. Three more pages and I'd finished.

I tied the curtains back. The sky was a gray broth, and off to the east the broth gathered, simmered, thickened; ready to boil into daylight. I dressed and went down the hall to the music room, and seating myself at the piano, began to play in the thin light. But the room felt wrong: Beethoven felt wrong. Phrases from Twilah's deposition ran through my head.

"Sponge bath . . . bed rail down . . ."

Marguerite Cleary, the absent woman, had attended Twilah in the convalescent home and left the bed rail down. Twilah rolled onto her side, fell to the floor, and broke her hip. When she sued the convalescent home, Marguerite Cleary left town. That's why all the stuff was still here in the apartment. She'd left in a hurry and had no time to pack.

I got up from the piano and wandered back along the hall. Vacant rooms on either side of me smelled moldy, rancid. Twilah had taken a desperate fall out of a hospital bed. Marguerite Cleary had neglected a patient and then left town. I felt like the worst parts of Twilah and Marguerite combined: convalescent, transient, neglectful. The hotel draws lost souls, Twilah had said. I'd given up not only my family, but my soul. I went to the hook behind the kitchen door and got my coat. Noted the starfish on my way downstairs. Closed the street door behind me. Turned the key in the lock and walked toward town.

"Good morning, Mr. Raithel," I said as I entered the second-hand music shop. He nodded his head and coughed. Instead of going to the classical music shelf, I pretended to be interested in a set of used drums near the cash register. He looked at me shrewdly.

"Taken up drumming, have you?"

I smiled and thumped a drumhead. "Do you ever take coffee breaks, Mr. Raithel?"

"Not hardly ever," he said.

"Will you have a cup of coffee with me?"

He didn't seem surprised. Nothing surprised him. He climbed down off the stool and made his way to the coat tree in the corner of the store where he wrapped a plaid scarf around his leathery neck, put on his coat, and added a blue baseball cap. 'Fiddlin' Fool', it said over the bill. He closed the door without locking it and we crossed the street to Mom's.

"Do you play the violin?" I asked, eyeing his hat as we settled into a booth under a braid of plastic garlic. The tired-looking waitress smiled and asked us how we were.

"Nah, I don't play violin," he said. "I play fiddle."

"Where do you play?"

"Square-dances. Talent show at the Grange. Anywheres they ask me." He looked at me keenly. "Not shopping for music today?"

"Not today." The waitress filled our coffee cups. Mr. Raithel coughed. He wiped his mouth with a large handkerchief and watched me milk the spotted cow, an acquired skill I'd grown rather proud of.

"Cream?" I asked. He nodded and I lined up my shot. "Do you ever see the piano teacher in town?" I asked.

Mr. Raithel swirled his cup and pondered. "You mean the lady I told you about?"

"Twilah Chan. You probably knew her as Twilah Reynolds."

He shrugged, a gesture that almost started another cough. "I wouldn't recognize her, it's been so long." He spoke carefully to keep a balance in his chest. "She buys her music somewheres else."

"She comes down to the hotel and gives me lessons," I said. "She remembers the piano from years ago. Not a very good piano"—I waited for him to hawk— "but we both think you did a fine job tuning it."

"My dad taught me to tune the piano," he said between breaths, and he was off on a story about riding in the wagon to Vernon one Saturday when he was a boy to watch his dad tune pianos in six churches. "It was sure a long day."

"Twilah Reynolds Chan hasn't lived in the old hotel for years," I said.

"There's a square-dance at the Grange Saturday night," he said. "I'll be playing if you care to come."

"Thank you. But I don't square-dance."

"Oh, they love to have people come and watch." The bell on the door tinkled. A group of shipyard workers came in on morning break.

"I guess Twilah Reynolds Chan had hip surgery and was in the convalescent home quite a long time," I said.

"Dunno." He stirred his coffee. "You'd enjoy those square-dances." He looked at me over the rim of his cup and slurped.

"I don't even know where the Grange is," I said.

"Easy. You know where the old drive-in sits? You take a left . . ." I listened to directions.

"Twilah Reynolds Chan hasn't been married very long, I don't think," I said. I turned my cup once in its saucer.

"You're studying classical music and that's a long way from fiddlin'." Mr. Raithel moved the salt shaker closer to the pepper, then back away. "But music's music. And people are people. You've got the tall, you've got the short," he said, unfolding his paper napkin and folding it up again. "You've got the people who stay and you've got the people who move on." He coughed. "Your piano teacher stayed. The little nurse from the rest home"— he looked at me shrewdly—"the one who lived in the old hotel, she's gone. Left. Skidaddled."

He'd known all along what I was talking about.

The waitress poured coffee for the shipyard workers, then plodded to the table in the corner and returned the coffee pot to the hot plate. Her face was impassive and without questions. Her hairnet restricted her hair and possibly her thoughts. For a moment I wanted a hairnet, too. I would rather be tired, have tight hair, and live with my children than be rested, free, and living away from them. I'd made a mistake in divorcing Ron, and another when I left Seattle for Hilliard.

"Mr. Raithel, what do you know about Twilah Chan and Marguerite Cleary?"

"Just what was in the papers. The town got a little worked up for a while, and then everything settled down again. That's the way it always happens."

"What was the town worked up about?"

"Your music teacher fell out of bed at the rest home and claimed the young nurse left the railing down on purpose. 'Course, the young nurse said she didn't. Still, she left town, which didn't look good."

"Who do you believe?"

"Dunno."

I leaned into the table. "Did anybody try to find Marguerite Cleary? Did anybody get her side of the story?"

"That, I don't know."

The conversation stalled. "What do you think about people who leave town?" I asked.

"Depends on what they're leaving. And why."

"A family, for instance."

"We're supposed to leave our parents," he said.

"What if you leave your children?"

He coughed. "How old are they?"

"Eight and nine."

"Not supposed to do that," he said. He shot me a keen look. "Depends."

"On what?"

"On the circumstances," he said. "Everything depends on the

circumstances." It was the kind of answer that could not make me feel better.

He smiled, all creased leather and missing ivory. "You have a lot of questions about right and wrong, Missy."

"Don't you have opinions, Mr. Raithel?"

"Not many."

"I saw a deposition transcript in my apartment."

"Don't know nothing about transcripts. They's only so many ways to dispute and only so many things to dispute about." He lifted his head and looked at me from the lower quadrant of his cataracts. "She's teaching you to play the piano. And she don't buy her music from me. That's what I know."

We sat together for a while. I listened to him tell about his medical expenses and the class action suit for asbestos workers. Even Mr. Raithel was party to a lawsuit. As we left the booth, he hawked and said in a voice full of phlegm, "When you're young you can walk away from things. When you're old, you can't get away so easy."

19

"Hi, Mom!" Lawrence said over the telephone. "We won the soccer game!"

"Congratulations!"

"The coach let me play the last half. And guess what?" Even over the telephone Lawrence managed to sound both humble and impressed. "I made an assist."

"Lawrence, I'm so proud of you. I wish I could have been there."

He was silent before slipping back into a pose. "Yeah, the pressure was really on." In the background Matthew carried on a conversation with someone: not Ron, I thought.

"Who's there?" He grew quiet. "Who's Matt talking to?"

"Anna."

"Who's Anna?"

"Our babysitter."

"Does she come after school?"

"No, she lives here."

"How old is she?"

Lawrence was suddenly cautious. "She's a grown-up."

We waited for each other to speak.

"Do you like her?"

"She's okay." Then, in his own grown-up manner, he changed the subject. "How's everything in Hilliard?"

"Just fine."

"When are you coming home for good? Back to Seattle, I mean."

"In a few weeks. I'm coming to see you on Friday. Want to drive back to Hilliard with me for the weekend?"

He didn't say yes.

"Can I persuade you? There's no soccer game this weekend . . ."

"Yeah, but . . ."

"But you don't like Hilliard."

"We don't know anybody."

"The three of us can just talk, go to the indoor swimming pool, walk on the beach. It will be nice." Silence. "It's part of the schedule," I reminded him. "Dad and I planned it ahead of time. Hasn't he told you?"

"Not yet."

"Well, he's probably forgotten to mention it. Give it some thought." Silence. "I'll see you, anyway, on Friday."

Anna wasn't at the house when I got there. Neither was Ron. I heard Matt and Lawrence playing touch football in the backyard with kids from the neighborhood. I lifted the string on the side gate and squeezed between the garbage cans and fence. The ping-pong table was still set up on the covered patio: it was old and warped.

I reached the backyard and waved to the boys. The game slowed for a few seconds while everyone adjusted to being watched. When play resumed, the moves were flamboyant and a little out of control. Gradually the glances in my direction grew further apart, and pretty soon everyone forgot I was there.

I moved a lawn chair behind the imaginary end line and sat down with my coat on, feeling like an intruder in my old home. But the scrambling in the grass, the smells of my neighbor's dinner (she was still ahead of the rest of us, her dinners served precisely at six, casserole in the oven by five) lulled me into a state of peace. Credit, blame, all judgments and opinions, all felt unimportant. The gods watched, entertained and kind.

The backyard play dwindled and ended. I didn't immediately

follow the boys into the house, but remained in my old backyard that seemed to have expanded since I first sat down. A fresh, new light washed the neighborhood. In the background, the sound of Chopsticks being banged out on the piano by children was like a promise of music that exists somewhere else, speeding toward us from a star whose light we've learned to see but with whose music we aren't acquainted.

When I crossed to the house, I found Matt and a friend perched on the piano bench.

"Let's hear that again," I said. Standing, flexing my knees until my hands were nearly level with the keyboard, I started an accompaniment, octaves and chords, to their treble. When we finished I showed them how to play 'Heart and Soul' and we embarked on another noisy duet.

The friends went home but Matt and Lawrence and I remained at the piano together, wrapped in music, playing and singing from a Xeroxed music sheet one of them had gotten at school. "Oh, ye'll take the high road and I'll take the low road," we sang.

"Bring the music with us," I suggested, "and some other songs, too. We can play and sing in the old hotel."

"You don't have a piano."

"Wanna bet?"

"Where?"

"You'll have to find it."

"Which floor is it on?"

"I can't remember," I said. "It's such a big building. So many floors. And on every floor, so many rooms." I'd hooked them. Hilliard had a piano and possibilities and mysteries.

When they went upstairs to pack for the weekend, I sat down on one end of the sofa and looked around. The living room was recently rearranged. For a year and a half everything had remained as it was before I'd left, but now I noticed the easy chair and rocker had changed places. The painting I'd given Ron, geometric shapes on a pale background, was replaced with an illustration of a bearded man fishing in a swift, dark river that swirled about his hip boots.

"You got the key?" yelled Matt.

"Bring the soccer ball!"

"Leave a note for Dad!"

While they shut the back and side doors, I walked into the kitchen—another woman's kitchen now—and laid my child support payment on the counter. I anchored the corner of the envelope under the cookie jar and lifted the lid. Oatmeal raisin. Homemade. I used to make cookies; now I paid child support. I took a pen from my purse and wrote Ron's name on the envelope while the kids tramped through the kitchen on their way out the front door. I lifted my chin and followed. In spite of risk, loss, and another woman's cookies, I was not sorry to be earning my own living, and a good one at that. Well, it had been a good one until I took the leave of absence and it would be good again, as soon as I returned to the city.

North of Seattle I began to feel festive: mother and sons together again.

The next day, Saturday, when we were cutting through the park under a five-o'clock winter sky, with our hair slicked back from a swim at the indoor pool and the faint smell of chlorine coming off our skin, we seemed foreign to each other.

Lawrence stopped to examine the old fighter plane installed on the playground by the City. Matthew, a fifth-grader, at first ignored anything having to do with play equipment. But the metallic sheen in the dying light proved too much and he joined his younger brother in the open cockpit. I sat down on a park bench with our gym bags. My mood was like the sky: end-of-the-day mixed with fast-moving clouds. The boys and I had just about as much of their childhood left as the day had light. The bright, hot sun of their babyhood and of our unscathed little family had already sunk. I watched them climb onto the swept wing. Their faces in the stormy, gray-green light looked older and less familiar; these were two young fighter pilots I barely knew.

"It's almost dark," I called out after they'd made their umpteenth trip along the fuselage. "Ready to go?"

They slid onto the wing, jumped off its tip, and joined me on the dirt path leading through a stand of lodgepole pines toward the bandstand at the far end of the park. Lawrence stopped to change his gym bag from one shoulder to the other. I watched the pine boughs stir and scratch across the low moon's face. Just as the kids started swinging along with their bags again, a voice spoke from the trees.

"You all have any change?"

I jumped. Someone stood in the shadows and I squinted to see, aware that the boys were standing very still, frozen. She was a big woman, leaning on a grocery cart. She was wearing more than one winter coat, and a turban covered her large head. She was black and her dark eyes, set in brilliant white, focused deeply on mine.

"You all got some change?" she repeated. I reached for my purse.

"Nice children," she said matter-of-factly, looking at the boys.

"Yes," I said. The kids were staring at her. Matthew pulled on my arm.

"Can't make no living in this town," the woman said, shifting her weight from one leg to the other. "You got any work for me?"

I shook my head. "I've just moved here, myself." The boys had gone a few steps ahead. They stopped and turned to watch me give her two dollars.

"What do you do?" I asked, zipping up my shoulder bag.

"Cook and clean." She threw back her turbaned head and looked up at the night sky. "I be out here again tonight."

"Good luck to you," I said. The boys almost ran the last few steps out of the park. Their hair, dry now, shone under the streetlight at the corner.

Matthew spoke with authority. "You shouldn't talk to strangers, Mom."

"I kept my distance," I said. "She caught me by surprise." I liked the woman. Her kind—gentle—expression and lonely endurance affected me. But I couldn't expect the boys to understand why anyone would be in the Hilliard park on a cold night pushing a cartful of odds and ends. They were eight and nine and had never been hungry.

"How much money do you get for your allowance?" I asked. They rolled their eyes. *Here she goes.*

"Answer me."

"Ten dollars a week. But we have to work for it."

"Do you buy your food?"

"No."

"Clothes?"

"No."

"Pay rent?"

"No."

"She probably earns twenty-five dollars on a day that she finds work," I said. "On that she can never get ahead."

"You still shouldn't talk to strangers."

"How else am I going to learn anything?" But I wouldn't try to undermine their dad, their teachers, the media, everyone who told them strangers were kidnappers, murderers, and sex perverts.

"I kept my distance," I repeated. "And yes, one has to be careful. Still, it's good to keep an open mind." Silence. "To understand yourself and others, you need to keep an open mind."

"Dad understands things," said Matthew, "and *he* doesn't have an open mind."

Lawrence changed the subject. "I don't want to be poor like that lady," he said.

"Neither do I. But it could happen." They both looked alarmed, as if I'd uttered a plan for the future. "I might lose my job for some reason," I said. "Get sick, maybe. Get old. Fail to keep up with the times. Get fired. Recession. Banks go under. Lots of reasons why people are poor."

"Dad will never lose his job," said Lawrence.

"He's got tenure," Matthew said.

"And insurance," added Lawrence. "Lots of it."

"It costs him an arm and a leg," said Matt.

"We'll never be poor," said Lawrence, sounding unsure in spite of himself.

"Nobody sets out to be poor," I said. But they didn't want to hear more, and they sped up and walked ahead. After a few minutes they slowed their pace and dropped back beside me. I put a hand on each boy and left it there: Lawrence put his arm around me and Matthew matched his steps to mine.

"I love you guys," I said.

"Why don't you come back?" said Lawrence, giving me a squeeze around the waist. "You wouldn't have to live in a hotel and climb all those stairs. You wouldn't have to walk so far to the piano. And we wouldn't have to come to Hilliard."

"I will be back by your birthdays, remember? I told you that before I left."

"He means come back to our house," said Matthew in a low voice. He moved away from my hand. "He means come home." The edge of Matt's pain sliced through me.

"Yeah. Dad and Anna fight all the time," added Lawrence. "She talks too much when he's trying to read. She smokes a lot. Dad has to empty the ashtrays."

I was ashamed of the glee that cheapened me: *no one can take my place*. Ron always did underestimate me.

"The important thing is, how does she treat *you*?"

Both boys shrugged their shoulders as if it were none of my business.

"Daddy and I have worked everything out," I reminded them. "We don't live together anymore." Mist swirled about our faces now and hung under the streetlights. "Pull your hoods up, boys. The weather's changing. If Dad and Anna are fighting," I continued, "maybe you'd like to stay with me for a while."

"In Hilliard?"

"Well, it's not so bad here," I replied, strangely offended. "And remember. I'll be back in Seattle soon. If Daddy and I agree—I'm not saying we will— but if we agree to it, would you like to live with me for a while in Seattle?"

Dead silence as we walked through the bright strip of street near the lights in the boatyard.

"Anna's going to leave," Lawrence said.

"How do you know that?"

"She says so all the time."

"Well, that's up to her," I said.

"If we lived with you, we'd have to go to a different school," said Matthew. "It would be—inconvenient."

I laughed out loud. He had used Ron's intonation exactly. I hooted again. "Things can't be all that bad at home," I said, "if you're concerned about convenience."

They smiled sheepishly. I reached to ruffle their hair, found their hoods instead, and so I ruffled their hoods. "Nice try, guys," I said, sounding, I thought, modern. Laid back. Like Anna probably was. The boys skipped a few steps, ran on down the block, and finally stopped to wait for me at the display window of the hardware store. They didn't need me as much as I—or they—thought. It was I who needed them.

20

The channel shone gray and limpid as I walked behind the abandoned cannery and onto the gravel beach. Masts against the streaked sunset looked like stems and flags of musical notes. Pink-and-orange clouds behind the rigging moved to a fast tempo, and the halyards chimed. Soon the foghorn would begin blowing its low A.

Greg lived on a wooden sailboat moored at the docks just below the old hotel. From the beach I saw him bailing out his dinghy beside the boat. Walking toward the water, I passed a tug tied up one space away and approached the sloop: THUNDER. Wearing bright yellow rubber boots up to his knees, a sweater and heavy flannel jacket, he seemed untouched by the damp and cold.

"Couldn't put it off any longer," he said. He was using a half-gallon can to dump the water. Beyond the channel, out in the sound, an ominous dark line marked wind and rough water. During dinner at the Cabbage Patch and two outings in his sailboat, Greg had taught me some elementary facts about weather up here.

"I didn't think it had rained that much," I said, eyeing the level of water in the dinghy.

"You'd be surprised." Greg didn't give out much opinion. If he were asked, 'What do you think the weather will do?' he would look up at the sky and say, 'Whatever she wants. Maybe rain.'

He worked silently.

"I just had a piano lesson with your mom," I told him. He nodded. "My head is full of Beethoven. I'm memorizing a sonata, and if I make any sudden movement, the notes will fall out of place."

He grinned and kept on bailing.

"Coffee's made," he said after a while. I went around to what I'd learned to call the port side and stepped over into the cockpit. Down-channel, the little ferry to Guemes Island set out on its ten-minute run; a fishing boat rounded the point from the bay, engine running rough. Everything had to come and go through this narrow, deep channel and the ferry had the right-of-way.

I poured coffee and sat down at the built-in table. Above my left ear, a net bag gently swung with the movement of the boat. The woodburner hummed. The automatic bilge came on, groaned, and emptied.

THUNDER had been Greg's home for several years. He'd sold his fishing boat, gone to Mexico, lived there for a while, come back, bought THUNDER, set up a blacksmith shop on property he owned a few miles outside of Hilliard, and traveled back and forth between the channel and Cedar Forge, as he called his shop, in his old pickup.

Soon the rhythmic splashing of the bailer stopped and I felt THUNDER list as Greg stepped into the cockpit. His lean thighs and bright yellow boots were all I could see. He removed the boots, setting them on slats in the deck, and climbed down into the cabin. While they dripped into the bilge, he poured himself coffee and sat on the step, drawing warmth from the woodburner beside him. Between one sip and another he reached over to a drawer beneath the built-in bookcase and pulled out a bracelet of polished steel with fine black striations running through it. He laid it on the table in front of me.

"It's lovely," I said.

"Damascus steel."

"How do you make the lines?"

"Pound like hell." He smiled and scooted onto the banquette

beside me. The bracelet stayed on the table. Water lapped at the hull.

"How's the old hotel?" he asked.

"Good." I was surprised that the building, creaking at night in the wind and rain, didn't frighten me. In the old hotel there was room to stretch. "There, I'm free."

Greg didn't ask why I liked being free. He'd never asked why I was alone. He'd never quoted the homily that always filled me with guilt: 'Bloom where you're planted.' *We have legs*, I was primed to retort. *Not roots.*

"That's why I have a boat *and* a shop," he said. He reached over to replace the bracelet in the drawer and leaned back with his cup of coffee. I felt accepted, and leaned back beside him.

21

The folk crafts fair was held every year at the county fairgrounds, halfway between Christmas and Easter, Greg said, when everyone needs encouragement. People drove up from Seattle, came from the islands by ferry, traveled from as far north as Bellingham and farther: even Canada.

Twilah, Arturo, and I squeezed past the entrance booth with the crowd. Behind us the shuttle bus threw out white dust as it turned in the gravel lot for a last run to the ferry dock. We had come ten miles outside city limits to a hillside overlooking the reservoir where spruce and Douglas fir dropped their needles onto the County grounds, making a rich mulch for fair-goers to scuff through. The spicy, patrician scent of evergreens floated above lower smells of livestock and hand-pulled taffy coming off the fairway. The sky was luminous gray, with a wet, blue-black look to the north.

I'd decided to forget Twilah's snub at the Christmas party. There was too much to be learned from her and I had no other teacher. Like a child who gets only one mother, I had little choice and took nourishment from her.

"Fairs seem medieval," Arturo remarked as we entered the main events building.

"It's a wonderful old tradition, the fair," agreed Twilah, clearing a path with her clogs. Behind her, her long gingham skirt swept a few inches above the sawdust floor. We circled the hall, examining displays of pottery, leatherwork, handmade soap, tatting.

"Where's the metalwork?" I asked as we began our second round. I had not seen Greg's booth.

"They always put the forges outside," Twilah said. "Fire code, I presume."

Arturo had stopped to examine a quilt, a pattern called Rocky Road Home. Lifting the edge with one finger, he studied the bright patchwork with private concentration. Surrounded by folk crafts of the Northwest, he seemed profoundly Chinese, his quality quite unlike the hearty energy of the bearded men and long-skirted women selling their wares.

Twilah watched him, too. If she thought he looked wistful or sad as he fingered the quilt, she did not show it. He turned away from the patchwork and glanced around for her. They stepped close and touched hands. I imagined them at night, alive with erotic touching in bed before falling into a deep and peaceful sleep.

Two booths farther on, a basketmaker sat on a low stool beside a tub of stripped blackberry vines soaking in water. He lifted his head once and smiled. I bought a basket from him, then looked for the Chans. Soon I saw a lean and sleek and copper man; saw a high-boned, snap-eyed woman. There were none at the fair so distinctive as they. I watched for a moment and then joined them.

"Let's go see the sheep and long-haired rabbits," said Twilah.

The smell of warm manure reached us as we crossed an open area, stepped up, then down onto the straw-covered floor of the next building. At one side of the barn-like hall, sheep stood in pens. On the opposite side, along a raised wooden platform that ran the length of the building, carders, spinners, weavers, and knitters sat working behind their goods tables.

A nasal cry ripped the air. The crowd moved forward as a bearded man in a short leather apron dragged a sheep to the roped-off center of the hall. A woman standing behind the rope held a stopwatch and electric clippers. In what seemed like one motion, the man in the apron passed her, grabbed the clippers, plunged into the ring, threw the sheep to the floor, pinning it there with one knee. The clippers buzzed. Wool mat peeled off the sheep's pink hide. The man knelt lower, leaned on the hind quarters with his knee, lifted one of the sheep's legs, lifted another, buzzed down the belly, over a flank, around the anus, straight up the back like a bulldozer through brush, until he jerked the clippers free, and jumped to his feet. The sheep lumbered up, and the rite was finished.

"Two minutes and fifty-eight seconds!" announced the woman with the stopwatch. Someone rushed the wool across the room.

"It's the sheep-to-shawl contest," Twilah said, her face flushed. "Now it's up to the carders."

Arturo had wandered off. We found him at the far end of the barn, standing quietly in front of a spinning wheel where an unsmiling woman pulled and treadled, treadled and pulled. Behind us, young 4-H Club members led their lambs around a ring past the judge, a large woman who, herself, resembled mutton.

"Shall we look for the blacksmiths?" I suggested.

"Indeed, let's." A wet wind had come up, stirring the evergreens: fir boughs bobbed lightly and rubbed against each other, releasing their sweet, pitch scent. Plastic tarps over the blacksmiths' booths snapped. Greg's forge glowed. A small crowd had gathered, and I stood on tiptoe to see over the people in front. He was showing them how to make a chisel out of steel rod. He heated it in the fire, pulled it out fast, hammered the soft, red-hot mass, then plunged it in a bucket of water where it sizzled and fried.

He had a line of patter as he worked. "Ladies and gentlemen, we've heated it. We've drawn out the point"—he looked up from his work and saw me, and wiped sweat off his face with the back of one arm—"we've drawn it out by hammering. Now we'll heat it again, quench it in water to harden it"—he showed us the chisel dripping from the tub—"and slowly reheat, bringing it to a light straw color where we want it hard; dark straw for the softer surface. We'll quench it at bronze."

People craned their necks to see.

"He could have been an artist instead of a blacksmith," Twilah said. "A sculptor."

"But he *is* an artist," I said.

"Is that for sale?" she called out when Greg had straightened up again. He hesitated.

"Everything's for sale," he said.

"I'll offer you five dollars." she said.

"Ten," said the man in front of me.

"Ten, on the way to fifteen. Name your price," said Greg, taking up his patter again.

I glanced at Twilah, expecting her to offer more. Her bony, aristocratic, beautiful face was set: stubborn. It seemed odd for her to stand on such a low offer, and I thought maybe she had only wanted to get the bidding started. Greg moved his safety glasses up onto his curly hair and scanned the crowd. His eyes flicked to his mother's and away.

"Fifteen," I said. Twilah jerked her head toward me. The forge blazed up and Greg stooped to regulate it. His safety glasses slipped.

"Sold," he said, and handed down the chisel. Not that I had ever really wanted a chisel. Twilah turned her back on me and moved away.

"Ma'am, you have just purchased a fine, hand-forged piece of steel," Greg said, but his eyes were on his mother who had begun pushing through the spectators. I watched Greg's demonstration a few minutes longer, then followed Twilah down the fairway where she turned her head this way and that, looking for Arturo who, apparently, had wandered off again.

This time we found him—I was walking several steps behind her—seated at a table behind a teapot and four cups and saucers. For a moment I wondered if he'd brought them from home. Who but Arturo would find cups and saucers at a fairground? But no, it was a concession run by a church group: women were serving polite refreshments out in the wet breeze, not far from smells of sheep and rabbit and hot iron. We sat down on either side of Arturo. I was careful not to speak. I laid—hid—the chisel on the ground under my chair.

"Every year the Martha Circle serves at the fair," Twilah said irritably. "The Lord's work. Of course, they charge for it."

"Quite reasonably," said Arturo, replacing the chipped lid on the dark green pot.

"Everything costs more than it should. I have to pay a fortune to get something from my own son." Arturo sent a swift look in her direction.

"I have no idea what blacksmiths charge for their work," I said, not sure where the conversation was going.

"It's just a tool," snapped Twilah. "Greg could have been a *sculptor*."

"Would you care for a cookie?" interrupted one of the women in the Martha Circle, holding out a plate to the three of us.

"Indeed, yes," said Arturo, behaving as though Twilah weren't furious and as if we weren't thirty feet from the pungent sheep pens.

"How much are they?" Twilah demanded.

"Twenty-five cents apiece." The woman seemed embarrassed. "It's not for us. It's for the mission." There was a moment of silence. "Snickerdoodles," she added.

"I'll have one," I said.

"Four snickerdoodles," Arturo said gravely. Silenced by Twilah's hostility, I watched Arturo pour the tea, strings and labels swaying. Under other circumstances it might have been fun to pretend this was a fragrant brew from Mainland China, shipped through Hong Kong or Macao, carried in sampans, the holds of freighters, black-marketed out of the east to this son of China now positioned imperturbably on the edge of the San Juan Islands. But Twilah's mood hung heavily over the table and I gave up the image. Arturo took a small bite of cookie; Twilah moistened hers in tea. I felt nervous and hungry, torn between the desire for large bites and impulse to imitate the Chans' daintier etiquette.

"Is this the church where you played the organ? Are these women Methodists?"

"Yes. And they've got tin ears. They prefer 'Whispering Hope' to Bach." She leaned over her cookie. "I played a Bach Capriccio for the postlude and had complaints!"

"Twilah has had a varied career here in Hilliard," offered Arturo, smoothly accommodating her anger and the social requirements of a tea party. He caught the eye of one of the ladies and lifted the lid of the pot to indicate we'd run out of hot water. "Much like mine."

"Varied career?"

"When I first met Twilah she was teaching piano and living in one room in the old hotel," said Arturo. "She'd just lost her father and sister in an automobile accident. Greg was ten." I glanced at Twilah. The bony forehead, nose and jaw line was hard, but the expression had begun to soften.

"You've known each other for years, then."

"Of course," said Twilah.

"Your last name, 'Chan,' " I said. "It's new, isn't it?"

"Arturo rescued me from the convalescent home," said Twilah. "From an illness and . . . negligent treatment. He brought me to his apartment and took care of me. We married."

I was curious about how they met and about the father's and sister's accident. I wanted to know why they'd decided to get married. But he'd stopped talking again.

"You were a guest, then?" I asked him. They both looked blank. "In the old hotel? When you met Twilah?"

"Well, one might say that." Arturo returned to his tea and cookie. I had gone too far. The over-eager, large-footed western woman who was not quite subtle enough for far eastern gentleman. I polished off my snickerdoodle and sat with my hands in my lap, discouraged.

He set his cup soundlessly in its saucer.

"It was 1955." His wife leaned back in her chair. I leaned forward. "I had been living in Costa Rica for a very long time, helping my parents in their restaurant. I was then a man of thirty, and I had nothing to show for my thirty years of living except a few stories and articles published in the small Chinese language newspaper in San José; they were also passed from hand to hand in China by a friend of my father's." A Martha Circle woman came to our table with more water for the teapot.

"I decided to seek my fortune away from my family," he continued after refilling all cups. "I had always wanted to write and teach. My father's oldest brother emigrated to Canada as a student in 1917. He gained a degree and was teaching at a college in Vancouver." Arturo slowly lifted his tea bag in and out of his cup. "And so in 1955 I set out for British Columbia." There was a silence and he sipped his tea.

"Please go on," I said. "Please don't stop."

"I couldn't find my uncle," Arturo continued. "Every year or two he had written us from Vancouver. He told us he was teaching in a small college there. I went to the school and asked about him. They had never heard of him."

My teabag cooled in its water.

"I never did find him in Canada," Arturo said. "But after several months working as a waiter—the very occupation I left home to escape—I found someone who had known him." Again, the story stopped, there was a silence, and he sipped his tea.

"And did you find your father's brother?"

"I did."

"Where?"

He studied my face. "In Hilliard," he finally said. "In the old hotel."

I drew in a quick breath. "What floor was he on?"

"The high-most."

"Topmost," Twilah corrected him. "The topmost floor."

One of Arturo's sleek, thick hairs fell down over his forehead.

"What was your uncle doing in Hilliard?" I asked.

"Working in the cannery."

"The old man was in a very bad way," Twilah said. "No money. Sick."

"The Chinese have a saying." Arturo lifted his cup and set it down again. "The fallen leaf returns to the root." His calm gaze rested on Twilah's face.

"Chinese do not like to die away from China," she said.

"Was your uncle able to return home?"

Again Twilah answered. "He thought he *was* home. In China. All day and all night he sang Chinese songs."

"Children's songs," Arturo said. "Songs from the nursery. My father's brother died insane, far from China." Douglas fir needles rattled down on the tables. The breeze blowing paper napkins around the concession might have carried the wail of a defeated migrant; a transient.

Teatime had become hideous; the hotel I'd chosen to live in was abruptly terrifying. I wanted to grip my cup and swing it to my mouth. To slosh energy all over myself. To gargle and spit out the horror of failure, of emptiness, of dying alone in a strange place. But I controlled myself and set my cup in its saucer with the merest *chirp* of glaze on glaze.

"All is not tragic," insisted Twilah. "Arturo came for his uncle, and thus I met him on the same steps I climb twice a week for your piano lessons." She gazed at her husband, desire and respect playing across her features like changing light.

But Arturo blew his nose. "It is terrible to fail," he said.

The women of the Martha Circle were busy making up box lunches. The last person in the genteel assembly line inserted an apple as carefully as if it really mattered, closed the lid, tied up a ribbon, and added the box to a stack on the table.

Twilah looked from Arturo to me and back again. "Life goes on!" she declared. "The cost is high, but what choice do we have?" Arturo seemed preoccupied. She looked at me and said impulsively, "What do you think?"

"About what?"

"The cost." I thought of the forty dollars she charged me for an hour's music lesson.

"Perhaps a little high for the Hilliard market," I said, "but well worth it to me."

Or maybe she meant the chisel, in which case I might have said too low. She looked puzzled, but Greg was approaching and she didn't have time to ask what I meant. He sat down in the fourth chair, carefully, as someone does who has been sweating and isn't as clean as the people around him.

"Damn dentist," he said, and extended his plain green cup. Arturo poured.

"What do you mean?" said Twilah, forgetting about her bid and the chisel she'd lost. "What's happened?"

"A dentist accused me of cheating," he said. "Just now." He waved away the snickerdoodles. "I was steam-casting my silver fuchsias. The guy sees me drop the casting flask in the tub of water. When I take out the mold he says, 'You're a fraud. I know what you're doing.'"

"'Well, what am I doing?' I say. 'You had a finished one in the tub and just exchanged them,' he says. 'I'm a dentist. I work with investment material all the time. You've got to have a vacuum pump to do that.' 'Sir,' I say, 'I've been doing this for years with water, a torch, and steam. Would you care to step over here and watch?'

"'It won't work,' he says. 'You've got to have a pump.'

"'How do you think they cast gold teeth in poor countries?' I say. 'When I was in Mexico and Central America, I personally saw a dentist work with steam. Steam only.'"

"That's true," Arturo said. "I know that to be true."

"Well," cried Twilah, "what did the dentist say to that?"

"'Primitive!' " Greg rapped his large, dirty knuckles against the edge of the table twice. "Big expert. Can't stand simplicity. Got to have a pump." He leaned back in his chair and, first checking under the table, threw out his long legs.

"Who was it?" Twilah exclaimed. "Just tell me what dentist, and I'll fix his teeth." Greg's anger broke and he rested his head on the back of the chair and laughed.

Arturo turned to me. "The dentist is a fool," he said. "Who could fail to appreciate such a simple, ingenious process? Greg actually casts the fuchsia from the blossom itself. It is a flower preserved forever in silver."

During this polite articulation Greg reached under my chair for the chisel. Twilah was still basking in the high spirits of a moment earlier and either didn't notice the chisel, or chose not to. Her son studied it closely, as if to assure himself he'd made a good tool. He set it back under my chair, smiled at me, and stood up.

"Time to sell some more iron," he said. He hadn't stayed more than ten minutes. Perhaps the entire dentist anecdote was Greg's way of distracting his mother, redirecting her anger away from himself. Her passion seemed quick and fluid. Whatever their dynamic, it was theirs: they'd forged—perhaps not so much differently from the blacksmithing Twilah disdained—their own relationship.

As Twilah waited for Arturo to pay the bill, I forgot about her cheap bid. I drew strength from her. Twilah would never be defeated; she would continue to laugh and fight with her son, to teach students, to make a home for Arturo against all odds. Arturo would never end like his uncle. Arturo would die where he wanted to, for Twilah would see to it. I brushed aside her imperfections and loved her again with the big, juicy relief of a student—no, a child who hasn't been abandoned after all. Her protection extended even to me. She would teach me everything she knew; everything

I'd always wanted to learn.

"Thank you!" I said to all of them, unable to hide my happiness.

"The honor is ours," replied Arturo, bowing slightly.

We got up and walked Greg back to his booth. The sky darkened. Soon a slanting rain was sweeping us down the fairway. Walking fast to keep up with my teacher, I was pushed by the wind, propelled toward the parking lot, the shuttle bus, the old hotel. I could hardly wait to get home, tear upstairs, and run down the hallway to my music room. I wouldn't need the electric heater anymore because, with Twilah's help, I was big enough and hot enough to heat the room all by myself.

22

BACK IN SEATTLE the woman named Anna was on the porch washing windows.

"Hello," I said. "I'm Virginia Johnstone, Lawrence and Matthew's mother." Matthew. Lawrence. Johnstone. Sons. Mother. Had been the wife. Used to be somebody. Am not yet quite somebody. May some day be somebody. The words were crutches and I put my weight on them when I saw Anna singing at her work. She seemed earthy, comfortable, with a warm bronze color to her skin; suntanned in February.

"Hi," she said, looking down from the top rung of the stepladder.

"Are the boys in?"

"They're upstairs." She came down from the ladder. Her faded Levis fit well, and she had nice hips. I followed her into the hallway.

"Kids!" she shouted. "Your mom's here!"

"Next time I'll phone when I hit town," I said, trying to sound casual and likeable. It would have been easier if she was a bitch, if she was phony, jealous, insecure. Anything but this contented and basic woman.

Finally we heard the boys thump down the stairs. They rounded the landing.

"How are you, boys?"

"Hi, mom." They were perfectly natural, but my face was warm.

"Care to come in?" Anna asked. We followed her into the kitchen. She'd repainted it: to music, no doubt, and looking good in paint-spotted bib overalls and a painter's billed cap. The boys must love her. Ron must love her. For she is loveable. I sat down at the table amid the sounds and smells of a percolating coffeemaker. There was always hot coffee in the house now.

Ron and I never owned a coffeemaker. We'd made instant.

Anna pulled out cigarettes and an ashtray. The kids turned on the TV in the next room. It was louder than necessary. I thought perhaps the boys watched more television than was good for them. I followed them to the doorway.

"Are you packed?"

"How do you like Hilliard?" Anna asked in a comfortable, sexy, smoker's voice.

"A nice change. It's a quiet town."

"What do you do for fun?"

"Play the piano. Visit a couple of friends. Walk a lot." It sounded dull even to me.

"Do you have a car?"

"Sure," I said instead of 'yes'. The boys came back into the kitchen, bickering over the TV guide. I put out my hand to quiet them, a reflex.

"Matt and Larry told me you're a great piano player," Anna said. I looked at my son. Larry?

"I take it seriously," I said, putting an arm around each boy. That was my key quality. I was serious. Ron had found a woman who was comfortable, and while I struggled for identity, for achievement, the Annas of the world were either happily occupied or kicking back. Maybe I could be that way some day. But I'd have to work at it seriously.

"Let's hit the road," I said. "You don't want to miss any of the excitement in Hilliard."

"Right."

"Sure, Mom."

They rolled their eyes and left to get their packs. Anna got comfortable in one of the high kitchen chairs at the breakfast bar. Ron and I had looked hard for those chairs, and they were just the right height for her. I set my cup by the sink.

"Bye, guys," she said when they'd staggered back downstairs, packed for an expedition.

"Bye."

"See you when you get back."

"Okay. Tell Chip I'll be home—" Lawrence looked up at me. "When will I be back?"

"Sunday," I said. "Late Sunday afternoon."

"—late Sunday afternoon," he finished.

"Will do," said Anna. "Have fun." I thanked her for the coffee and prepared to change worlds again. The boys and I got in the car and drove away from a house—no, a country, that used to be mine. It was foreign territory now. I was the stranger.

23

THE ABSENT WOMAN had covered the lampshade in the corner with rose-colored yarn. It was a fire risk, but the living room glowed. Greg and I sat close on the old upholstered sofa.

"My kids don't like coming to Hilliard," I said. "They're glad to see me, but never sorry to say good-bye."

Greg touched one of my earrings.

"Kids need to be left alone," he said. "Most of us are overmothered."

"Do you really think so?"

"I know so."

"What about latchkey children?"

"What about them?"

"They're certainly deprived."

"Only if everyone thinks so."

"At the least, they're not safe."

"The careless ones aren't."

"How old do they have to be before they're not careless?"

"I don't know," he admitted. He grinned, probably at my appalled expression. "I was happiest when my mom left me alone."

"But were you developing—properly?" Beyond the rose lamplight Lawrence, then Matthew, might have been bending down until the key on the string around their necks reached the keyhole.

Greg laughed and looked down at himself. "I don't know. You be the judge." His voice dropped. "Twilah's a great music teacher, but as a mother, she's stifling."

"That's because you're her son," I said. "She doesn't try to dominate *me*."

"Wait a while." Greg's high forehead, nose, and cheekbones laid the lower planes of his face in shadow. I didn't tell him that tonight his profile closely resembled his mother's. His personality, too, seemed craggy, laughing one minute, moody the next. His eyes were drawn again and again to the rose-colored light in the corner.

"I was supposed to be a musical child," he said.

"You didn't cooperate?"

"I couldn't carry a tune."

"She loves you anyway."

He shrugged. "She wants a sculptor instead of a blacksmith. She draws phony distinctions between art and craft."

"Along with a lot of other people," I said. But it struck the wrong note with him. He stood up, irritated

"Let's go out," he said. I walked toward the kitchen where our coats hung on hooks and he lagged behind. Swinging the door away from the wall, I got my coat and stuck one arm in a sleeve, groping behind me for the other. Now I was irritated, too. I hadn't come to Hilliard to walk on eggshells. Our footsteps echoed in the stairwell; at the bottom, I paused to move a starfish out of the way, placing it closer to the banister. When I bent over, the blood rushed to my head.

"I don't feel like going to the tavern," I said.

Greg passed me, opened the door, and stepped out onto the sidewalk. "What do you feel like doing?"

"I don't know." I fiddled with the steel key, turning it end over end. Greg remained where he was, hands in his pockets. A dog's bark carried from blocks away.

"Whatever we were talking about upstairs," he said, "just forget it."

We didn't look at each other. I locked the door and we walked up High Street. The air was sharp and cold, and stars littered the sky.

"We're each like one of those stars in the great, black night," I said, "burning hard." I sounded phony.

"You be a star," he said. "I'm a forge, and it's damn hard work." I peered at him as we passed a lighted shop window. He wasn't kidding. He walked with his head down, shoulders massed.

"Vulcan," I murmured. He suddenly threw up his hands. I jumped.

"Vulcan!" he yelled. He grabbed my hand and yanked on it. The tension between us broke. We ran across the street through a yellow light—in Hilliard no great risk—and whooped our way to the tavern, bumping into each other, laughing, stopping and starting, deliciously out of control.

We slid into a dark booth at the back of the bar and Greg pinned me into the corner against the wall. His cold face and cold jacket were like a blast of air from farther north. We kissed. His tongue pushed into my mouth and I moaned.

"Hey, now," the waitress said in an interested voice. "Do you want a drink or what?" She was a buxom woman in her forties, grinning down at us.

"How are you, Loomie?"

She set down the pile of clean ashtrays she was distributing and squeezed in beside us. Greg leaned his head back against the booth, put his free arm around her, and pulled her in. She liked him; he liked her; I liked them both. I was loosening up now and I wanted more of this laughter.

"I'd better get back to work," Loomie said. "You want the usual?" He nodded and she slid out of the booth.

"How'd we get so serious back at your place?"

"I have no idea," I said. "But I've spent far too much of my life being serious. I'm sick and tired of it." He laughed. "What's the fucking joke?" I said. He laughed harder.

Loomie brought us two Irish coffees. Greg took a slurp and then I licked whipped cream off his lips. He set down his hot glass cup and was all over me again. I almost climaxed in the booth and told him so.

On the way back to my rooms, we stopped in the doorway of the hardware store for a long kiss. At the top of the stairs, I put my hand on the newel post.

"Can you stay awhile?" He kissed me for an answer and followed me into the kitchen. As we hung our coats behind the door again he touched my hair and said, "You're beautiful tonight. So relaxed."

I grew tense. On the way to the bedroom, Greg lifted the curtain to the absent woman's studio and I stepped in, fishing for the string to the light bulb. When the light came on he looked at the murals, photographs, line drawings, without saying a word.

"The woman who lives here, it's her room," I explained.

"I thought *you* lived here."

"I do. Partly." I took his hand and led him to my bed. It looked narrow.

"You've got less room than I have in the fo'c's'le."

"Is it too narrow?"

"Nah," he said gruffly, then smiled and pulled me down. The blinking neon of the Bar Fly Tavern across the street beat on the window shade, and lights and noise from the swing shift in the boatyard made this end of town seem busier at night than it was during the day.

"Lights bother you?" I murmured.

"No." He shifted his shoulder, and I moved my arm. My left ear was against his heartbeat. We lay there. Too soon: I had invited him in too soon. A reminder of smoke and liquor lay in his clothes and on his skin.

There's a reminder of smoke and liquor in his clothes and on his skin, I heard myself thinking. A generator kicked on in the boatyard. I'd rather be in the boatyard than in bed: I'd rather be a boat just now, floating on water. Boats can't think; boats—

"Virginia?" Greg whispered.

"Yes?"

"Relax."

I sat up. "I think I got ahead of myself."

"Don't think," he said, and pulled me down again and kissed me. He encircled me with his arms, rolled over, and threw a warm, heavy leg over me. Got up on his elbows and put his hands under my head. He smiled. Just like that. It was simple. And when desire began to flow, slow and thin at first, then thicker, blood pumped too fast through a line, nearly bottlenecking us both, we took off our clothes and used my little bed until it was wide and deep, a boat-bed. And when the wind and current slowed, it seemed just the right size, and we held each other in from the edges, and slept till morning.

24

THE SEVEN-O'CLOCK WHISTLE blew for the early shift. I smiled and stretched. Greg had loved me last night, me, a difficult woman, a confused, prickly, defensive woman. A transient. I threw my arm around the large-hearted man who'd made me happy in my narrow bed, and kissed him with love and gratitude. While the shipyard crew welded and hammered, we made love again. At last Greg stretched, hit the floor, and said, "We're going to my shop."

"It could snow," he said as we walked to his pickup. "It might already have snowed out at the shop, away from the water."

City streets turned to county highways. Wild grass beside ditches stood stiff with frost. In the early morning light the countryside rested under a white, brittle glaze; a ceramic casing. We touched hands. At any moment, with a clink and a chime, the world might break into pieces, each one bright and sharp and cold.

We left asphalt for gravel. The pickup rode hard on its old shocks. Drainage ditches beside us were watery slashes in the ground, scabbed over by ice, and dead, red leaves lay under bare alders. We passed a cow lying in a white field, her large body and udder melting the frost, warming the pasture.

Cedar Forge, Greg called the barn converted into a blacksmith shop. He got out of the truck, unlocked a heavy padlock on the side of the building, and slid open the shop door. We stepped onto the sawdust floor of a cold room that smelled of steel and tools. He turned on the lights and baseboard heaters.

"It's not much, but it's home," he said. I followed him part way into the room and slowly turned full-circle. At the far end, lengths of steel rod leaned against a wall. Hammers, different sizes, different shapes, hung near the anvil. Safety glasses and welding hoods lay on a table. Above the work bench, a thick orange extension cord looped around a nail.

"Tools are better than money," said Greg. He went over to the bench and showed me an awl, chisel, eye punch. He hefted them in his hand and dropped them back in the slot where they hung by their handles.

I walked to the anvil and pulled an iron bolt out of a hole.

"You found the hardy in the hardy hole," he said, as if I'd achieved something. He turned on a hairdryer, inserted it into a narrow pipe, touched a cigarette lighter to the pipe's far end, opened the valve on the propane tank, and lit the forge. I watched it grow red hot.

"The forge isn't as big as I expected," I said.

"Doesn't need to be." Basically it was a wide metal pipe lined with insulation. The small, hot flame grew redder and redder. In a few minutes it had turned white: what Greg called white hot welding heat. "If it gets blue we're in trouble," he said, regulating the propane. "It'll melt the forge."

He showed me an ingenious device called an Oliver, the modern smith's substitute for an apprentice. He pushed the pedal with his foot and a hammer slammed down with a deafening ring.

"There used to be a boy to do this," he said. He released the Oliver. I braced for another blow, but he moved away and took a leather apron off a hook. "No one apprentices anymore," he continued, tying on the apron, "at least not for wages blacksmiths can afford. You have to learn, unpaid." He pulled on a pair of gloves with long leather cuffs. "Most people don't have the discipline to learn something hard like smithing." He looked at me. "Or piano." Our eyes locked, then broke away. He picked up a metal tube bent at one end into a flower.

"What is it?" I asked.

"Fleur de lys." He handed me the long, cold pipe. "This is the picket."

"You're making a fence?"

"Gate. For a customer."

"It's going to be beautiful," I said. "I'd like a gate like this."

"Have to have a house first." He took it over to the forge and stuck the flower in the flame. Swiftly he removed it from the heat and laid it on the anvil where he began hammering with short, hard blows. When he stopped, the silence rang. The piece went through many stages, each heating and cooling a notch up toward the perfect picket.

"How long have you taken piano lessons?"

I thought he'd forgotten I was there. "Five years."

"You're going to be a great musician when you grow up," he said.

I grinned. "I'm never going to grow up."

He struck another series of sharp blows. "I couldn't sit still for lessons when I was a kid," he said. "I was my mom's only failure."

"You didn't like the piano?"

"Nah. Didn't like being cooped up in the house."

"She's a good teacher," I said.

He carried the picket back to the forge.

"I saw a transcript in my apartment," I said impulsively. "It has your mother's name on it, and Marguerite Cleary's."

"Yeah. It's a lawsuit."

"I'm subletting my apartment from Marguerite Cleary," I said. I knew he knew. I'd told him at The Cabbage Patch.

"Yup."

"Your mom knows, too."

"Yup."

"She never mentioned the lawsuit to me. She's been coming to the hotel to give me lessons twice a week. We always have tea in Marguerite Cleary's kitchen, but she's never mentioned it."

"She probably figures—"

"—it's none of my business."

"Right."

"I've wanted to ask her, but—I didn't think it was any of my business."

"Marguerite Cleary upset my mother," Greg said, sighting down the length of the picket with one eye closed, "and if anyone ever upsets my mother, she does something about it."

"That can be a good quality," I said. "She'd do the same for you, right? She jumps to your defense, right?"

"Oh, yeah. Anyone attacks me, that's it for them."

"I haven't known her very long, but I think she'd jump to my defense, too," I said hopefully. He didn't answer right away. When he did, it was in a detached tone.

"Up to a point."

"What point is that?"

"Up to the point of her own self-interest." He laid the picket on the anvil and turned off the forge.

"That's reasonable," I said, disappointed. "That's reasonable." But I wasn't sincere. I wanted Twilah not only to teach me, but to leap to my defense: to love me, to mother me. "Everyone has self-interest. You have to have self-interest to stay alive."

"Look, it's snowing," Greg said. I moved with him to the windows at the back of the shop. Snowflakes, big and fluffy as breadcrumbs, piled up on the outside sill. "Let's walk the property."

Outside, snow brushed our faces like cloth.

"I go through two climates every time I make the trip from the boat to the shop," Greg said. "It's always colder away from the water."

We crossed a clearing, gloved hands touching, and entered the woods. It was dark and dry under the trees. The snow hadn't penetrated the Douglas firs. I followed him, breathing steam into the air, hearing only the occasional movement of a bird deep in the cold boughs above us. After several minutes he cut to another path. I tried to keep my steps as quiet as his. Eventually, from the white light moving toward us, I could see we were leaving the trees. We came out on a brushy slope dusted with snow, and began walking downhill. A pond lay at the bottom of the property, and several ducks swam near its edge, ignoring the snow that melted as soon as it hit the black, still water.

"I'll check the pumphouse as long as we're down here," Greg said.

While he hiked the few hundred yards to the shed, I lingered to watch the ducks, five of them, tread warily away from me, pedaling underwater with big orange feet. One duck, oblivious to the white, muffled world, turned upside down. With its bottom pointed up to the falling snow, it stuck its bill into the mud to feed. Who had taught it to do that? It's mother, probably.

Greg returned and stood beside me. Snow lay thick and white on his dark hair.

"The ducks act like it's just another day," he said. "It's really coming down . . ."

"Do you think it's snowing in Hilliard?"

"Don't know."

I wiggled my gloved fingers, limbering up with an arpeggio in the air. "I have a piano lesson at one o'clock."

He wiggled his fingers, too. "Better get in as many lessons as you can before Mom leaves."

"Is she going somewhere?"

"Yup."

I began to shiver. "Where?"

He was walking toward the truck. "Didn't she tell you? To Guatemala."

"Guatemala?"

"Guatemala."

"When?"

"I'm not sure. Probably in the next few weeks."

"Why?"

"You need to ask her."

"When will she be back?"

"I don't know. Sometimes she stays away for months."

The truck was covered with a shallow layer of snow. We got in and Greg started up the engine. The white landscape moved.

"Does she go there often?"

"Every year or so."

"Why?"

"She's got something in the forge. Something up her sleeve." He shook his head, unbelieving. "So help me, I want nothing to do with it."

"What is it?"

"Some money-making scheme."

"Doing what?"

"Don't know. Ever the entrepreneur."

"Importing native art?" I crossed my arms hard in front of me. I was going to lose my piano teacher. Several weeks seemed an eternity. Up here in Hilliard I was nothing without her; I was barely something *with* her.

"Importing native art, all right." He turned onto the paved county road.

"Has she imported the art in their apartment?"

"Oh, yeah. She's been importing all her life."

Why? I wanted to ask again.

"Did you travel with her when you were a boy?"

"Sometimes. But then I got smart and stayed with Arturo in Hilliard while she left town and did whatever she did."

I uncrossed my arms and leaned back in the seat. It felt like I was examining a witness; trying to find out to what he was a witness. I couldn't stop the questions.

"Has she lived with Arturo since you were a child?"

"Off and on. She always comes back to him."

"And he doesn't mind?"

"I don't think so. She's pretty intense. It gives him a chance to rest up."

"I'm asking a lot of questions," I said.

"Yes, you are."

"Can I ask another?"

He checked the gauges on the dash, as if to get their approval, and didn't say no.

"Tell me about your mother's stay in the convalescent home."

"She had a hip replacement. Then she got an infection in the hospital. She was at the convalescent home for weeks."

"She's strong," I said. "She got well."

"Yes, she did." He braked at a four-way stop, shifted, and rolled forward.

"How long was she in the convalescent home?"

"Quite a while. Why don't you ask *her* these questions? If you want to know more about her," he said, "you'd better ask her yourself."

His profile was craggy again. We were silent for the rest of the ride. In town he dropped me off at the old hotel. We didn't kiss good-bye. Returning to Hilliard had put him in another fine mood. Or maybe it had been my questions.

25

I INSERTED MY KEY into the lock and pushed open the door. The stairwell seemed steeper than usual: straight up. I bent to pick up a rough starfish from the bottom step, and turned it over in my hand. Water and food used to wash in and out of its supple underside. Now it was dried matter beyond change.

I laid the starfish back on the step and shook off Greg's mood. His mood was not my mood. I clearly saw the piano and straight chair upstairs waiting for me. I felt compelled to master arpeggios. To get under the skin of Beethoven's music. To please Twilah.

I took the steps two at a time, shaking starfish and timbers. Hurried to the tower room and turned on the electric heater. Ran back down the hall to my rooms. Threw newspaper and wood into my little potbellied stove. Set a match to it.

Went for a sweater. Walked through the living room. Lifted the curtain. Through the studio windows, behind the Bar Fly Tavern, I saw the ship's hull filling in, steel beams gracefully bent. Curve of the bow. The chine, Greg called it. Ship getting ready to plow water.

I turned back to the studio. So much stuff. So much beautiful, personal stuff. Mermaid. Photographs. Diaries. Everything out in the open. See everything. Use everything. No excuses.

I want a studio, too!

I flapped aside the hanging blanket. Ran to the kitchen. Flew down the hall.

Stop! Music room's cold! Heater's too small! Greg's pissed! Twilah's leaving! Hilliard's temporary! Not real life here! Play-act-

ing! Don't deserve it! Think of the children! So selfish!
 Oh, shut up. Sit on the chair. Get to work.

26

THE TEAKETTLE WAS NEARING THE BOIL when I heard Twilah open the door at street level and start upstairs. She reached the top and knocked once.

"Anybody home?"

A halo of outdoor air surrounded her. Her face was as colorless as always, with no heat wasted in the high nose and cheeks. All of it went to the eyes.

She challenged rather than consulted her wristwatch. "I walked it in twenty minutes," she said, and went over to the window to gaze down on the channel and the little ferry trundling toward the island. The broken rainspout outside flowed with a musical run.

"Do you spend hours at this window?" she asked.

"Quite a lot of time." An idea occurred to me. "But I'm just as likely to be watching the boatyard. You've probably seen the fishing boat they're building."

"I've glimpsed it from the music room."

I could show her the boat from Marguerite Cleary's room. The teakettle whistled and I lowered the flame.

"This end of Hilliard is not my favorite place, Virginia," she said tartly as she followed me out of the kitchen. I held the hanging blanket aside and she entered the studio. Her eyes narrowed; darted from shelf to shelf; settled on nothing. My eyes stayed on her eyes.

Twilah moved to the window and looked out at the boat. "Boats are so much larger than they seem," she said. "I always forget about the part that's under water."

I fingered a wall hanging, a knotted end of yarn poking through stretched burlap. I hoped Twilah would notice.

"It takes so long to build a boat," she said, still looking across the street, "and only minutes to sink it."

"Marguerite Cleary . . ." I picked at the yarn while I spoke the name out loud. "Marguerite Cleary—"

Twilah whirled on me and almost shouted: "But some of us refuse to sink!" I stood with the yarn between my fingers, stunned.

"They've tried to diminish me again and again! Sometimes I've almost disappeared! Over and over I've almost became invisible! But I always come back! I've got music! I'm still teaching! I've regained my health! I have Arturo! He's going to make money again! I'm going to see that we make money!" She threw back her head; her face held color now.

She quieted abruptly and aimed for the living room. I followed, speechless as she led me back to the kitchen. We sat down at the plain wood table. After pouring two cups of tea I gave up all pretense.

"Twilah," I said, "please tell me about Marguerite Cleary and you."

She eyed me over her teacup. "How about letting in some air?" As if I hadn't spoken. As if she hadn't been ranting and raving a minute earlier. I opened the window.

"I feel as if you and she have something to teach me," I said, and accidentally jarred the table when I sat back down. Twilah swiped at the spilled tea with a paper napkin. "Marguerite Cleary ran away from the trouble at the convalescent hospital, didn't she? She left her home and her studio"—I laid a flattened palm on the table—"this home and studio right here, and ran away."

Twilah looked at me. No, she assessed me.

"It's none of your business," she said. "Find your own answers."

For a minute I thought she'd slapped me. I rubbed my face, stricken. I turned in my chair until my back was toward her, and, like a thirty-four-year-old child, ran to the woman of my imagination; the woman in my thoughts for over twenty years; the mother who had loved me, read to me, sat beside me on the piano bench when my feet still swung above the pedals. The woman who left, who didn't tell me where she'd gone, and who never came back.

A mass of clouds blew in. The sun went away and Hilliard grew dark. I picked up my teacup and started toward the music room.

One of the doors off the long hall stood ajar. I didn't have to look to know which room it was. I smelled sour, stained mattresses. I smelled failures, people who go away and don't come back. People who don't explain what you need to know. I put one foot in front of the other, down the dark hallway. I tripped and kept walking.

There is no such thing as mothers, I thought to myself. Not for me, not for my children, not for Greg, not for anyone. It's only a wish. I reached the music room and threw myself onto the straight chair at the piano. I began to play Beethoven fast and loud, Beethoven and the piano would answer my questions; Beethoven would be my mother.

I didn't hear anyone go down the stairs. I didn't hear the street door close, or look out the window to see someone stride up High Street and disappear.

Later, when it was night, I went downstairs to lock the door. I closed it hard and turned the big steel key. Upstairs again, in bed, I glanced at the boat in the boatyard. Under the floodlights, it looked bleached and unreal. God, such a slow process. I couldn't wait for it anymore. I turned on my other side, stared into the dark for a few minutes, then fell into a heavy sleep without dreams.

27

"Wanna go to a blacksmith workshop east of the mountains this weekend?" Greg asked as we climbed the ramp from the boat dock. "We'll have to pitch a tent," he added.

"Good," I said. "I need physical activity."

"There'll be lots of that," he assured me. "Tools to carry. Food to fix. The country over there is flat and dry. Good for walking."

Rain followed us from Hilliard through the pass, but once we descended the eastern slope of the Cascades, the air was bright and clear.

"On the Road Again!" Greg sang off key, and he really couldn't carry a tune. We passed miles and miles of fencing, ate in diners, and stopped to admire old courthouses in town squares. The movie marquee in one town announced two events: Sunday morning services, and a Saturday night concert, Janet Blake Cochrane, pianist.

"There's an idea," said Greg, slowing in front of the theatre. "You can give a concert at the Roxie."

"I'm not ready for my debut yet."

"You're damn good," Greg said.

"You've never heard me."

"Mom says you're terrific."

"I'm good, but not good enough."

"Good enough for what?"

I rephrased. "I'm not as good as I can be."

"We're talking about playing the piano, aren't we?" he said.

"Yup," I said.

We reached the last street in town and slowed for a yield sign. A semi blew past. We entered the highway behind it and breathed diesel.

"I'm sorry about last weekend," he said. "Talking about my mother makes me mean."

I studied his profile: straight, high nose and smoky eyes with heavy lids. Head of curly black hair. The son of a sharp-tongued mother. He drummed the fingers of one hand on the steering wheel.

"Your mother wears combat boots," I said.

He turned and looked at me with his mouth open. Then he laughed. Neither of us wanted another argument.

"What's growing in these fields?" I asked. Green-and-black speckled farmland stretched to the horizon, miles of crop pushing through dirt.

"Winter wheat," he said. "Did you and my mom have a . . . falling out?"

"Not exactly," I said. "I wanted her to talk to me and she wouldn't."

"About what?"

"About Marguerite Cleary and the lawsuit."

"My mom's private," he said. His eyes stayed on the road. "What exactly did you want to know?"

"It's none of my business," I said.

"We've already established that."

I watched green shoots flow by and felt a low-grade trembling begin.

He put his hand on my knee. "What do you want to know?"

"Why Marguerite ran away." *And why I've run away.*

"Because of the lawsuit." He rolled his window down and adjusted the outside mirror. The wind rushed in and changed the climate of the cab until he rolled the window up again. "Why are you so interested in Marguerite Cleary?"

"Because"—my voice rose—"I ran away, too. Because you're not supposed to run away."

Greg looked uncomfortable, as if he thought I might slip into some sort of hysteria. He withdrew his hand from my knee.

"People run away for different reasons," he said. It's what old Mr. Raithel had said. "You think the lawsuit will explain everything you don't know?"

"It might help."

"You want my mom to tell you you're okay, Virginia?"

"I don't want anything from her except music lessons," I lied. Beneath the obligato of my thoughts, the truck hummed down the road, engine drone in the key of D.

"Women who leave look bad," I said.

"Marguerite's okay. She doesn't look bad to me."

"Did you know her?"

"I knew her. She's okay."

I turned to face him. "Tell me about her."

"What do you want to know?"

"Why did she leave?"

Ahead of us, an old tractor wobbled along, half on, half off the shoulder. Greg moved out into the passing lane.

"Frightened, I'd say."

"Frightened of what?"

"Of my mother. Of the convalescent hospital. Of testifying. Of the law."

"How old was she?"

He swung back to the righthand lane. "Your age. Still is, I guess."

"Did you go out with her?" It was something I'd never considered.

"Yes."

Were you in love? I wanted to ask.

"It's really none of my business," I said.

"Right." He drove. I looked at the farmland and pictured Marguerite Cleary with Greg, the two of them climbing the stairs to her rooms, my rooms, walking arm-in-arm through the kitchen, living room, studio, into the bedroom . . .

"Whose fault was it," I asked, "the accident in the convalescent home?" Anyone could have seen me shaking now. I couldn't control it. Greg slowed the truck and pulled off onto the shoulder. Behind us, the tractor we'd passed ground closer.

"It wasn't Marguerite's fault," he said quietly, putting his arms around me.

"Who's wrong?" I asked. "Who's lying?" The tractor sounded like blades advancing down a row. I curled my legs in the seat and buried my head in Greg's denim jacket.

"What?" Greg shouted over the noise.

"Who's lying?"

The tractor pulled out around us. I lifted my head. The world was nothing but racket. The enormous wheels were so close I could see dried mud in the treads.

"Mom's lying!" Greg yelled above the thrashing.

"Why would she lie?"

The tractor's upright exhaust belched smoke around the curve ahead. Its noise grew fainter and fainter and was finally replaced by the wind that blows musically over this high, flat country. We were once again alone on the silent highway.

Greg had loved the woman, all right, I thought to myself, and Twilah hadn't liked it.

"Did Marguerite love you?" I asked.

Greg turned his palm up and laced his fingers through mine. "I don't think so. She wouldn't have left if she did."

"You slept with her."

His expression was watchful.

I took my hand away. "When we were in her studio and you asked me about all her things—"

"I was never in her apartment."

I raised my eyebrows. "Oh. Then the boat?"

He didn't answer.

"I'm just jealous," I said. "Like your mom." I reached for his hand again. "It's stupid. I'm sorry."

Greg whistled tunelessly through his teeth and moved back behind the wheel. He started the engine.

"Lawsuits are expensive," I said, looking for a change of subject without actually changing the subject. "If Twilah loses, she may have to pay the convalescent home's legal fees."

"I hope to God it's thrown out of court or something." Greg rolled the truck onto the highway. "I hope her attorney gets tired of dinking around with it. It's got to be a weak case. There aren't any witnesses."

"And Arturo?" I said. "What does he think about all of this?"

"He's learned to be engrossed in his work."

"When I leave," I said after a mile or two, "it won't be because your mother scared me off. It will be for my kids."

Ahead of us the road stretched like a smooth story for people who know where they're going; a silver-and-gray plot that moves toward a good ending.

"Did Marguerite talk to you before she left?" I asked. "Did she say good-bye?"

"No."

I pictured her in the studio cutting paper, sketching, writing poetry, filling in her life with rich detail. By the time we'd covered another mile I thought I knew what she must have felt: panic. The bed rail down. Crack of a bone on the floor. Furious director. Questions. An investigative board. Waiting to testify. The mess with Twilah seeping into her relationship with Greg. Greg vacillating between his mother and her. Tension ruining their love life. Running back from THUNDER in the early morning hours, tripping on the docks to get to her cold rooms . . .

She'd run from the lawsuit, and run from Greg who couldn't

take sides. Run, also, from a low-paying job, thankless tasks, spoons to mouths, diapers to old thighs. She would never be back. The lawsuit would eventually be dropped and, after a few years, except for one or two people, no one would remember her at all.

Greg had lost her. Or his mother had lost her for him; or he hadn't tried hard enough to keep her. Whatever had happened, I could tell by his silence and the numbed look on his face that it had been a bitter experience.

28

The farmer-blacksmith walked over to the truck and shook Greg's hand through the open window.

"Park her in the pasture," he said, motioning to a field behind a barn so new the wood looked pink. We'd be winter camping, Greg had warned me, so I'd brought sweaters, lined jacket, boots, and long johns. We could, he said, use a small propane heater if we really needed to. He intimated that true winter campers wouldn't need to.

We set up the tent at the top of the field, then walked back down to the shop, a smaller, older building set behind the new barn. By now blacksmiths were arriving. There were lots of smiles and greetings and beefy handshakes.

"Babe's here," someone said. In the lower field, an old woman dressed in overalls, flannel shirt, and a red baseball cap dismounted from her ancient Silver Stream trailer.

"Is she a blacksmith?" I asked the host smith's wife, a sinewy woman who was flapping checkered cloths over plywood-and-saw-horse tables.

'No, but she comes to all the workshops. She's got a museum of ironwork on her ranch." Greg and several other blacksmiths went to the lower pasture to meet her. I walked back up to the truck for cheese and crackers, my contribution to the potluck. It seemed inadequate, but who doesn't like cheese and crackers? When I got back, the sinewy woman was stirring a huge pot of chile over a hotplate. She pointed to a pile of carrots and onions and told me to peel until I got tired.

Wet carrot scrapings bled orange onto butcher-paper while conversation flowed around me: knife sales of a blacksmith from Oregon; a destructive test on somebody's steel that indeed destroyed it and disqualified him from an exhibit; laughter, hobnobbing, hustling, haggling; bargains proposed and struck.

That night after dinner the sawhorse tables were cleared away to make room for the auction. A handsome man with a handlebar mustache—a retired Navy commander, Greg told me—climbed onto a stool at one end of the shop. Babe sat just below him on a folding chair, the metal money box in her lap. Two intrepid young guys had climbed up on a crossbeam where they sat swinging their legs above the commander's head and looking down on knives, metal jewelry, sculpture, even honey from someone's bees, all set out for auction. Greg explained that the proceeds went to the association.

"What'll you gimme?" the commander called to the smiths who stood on the sawdust floor or sat on benches around the edges of the room. I watched him drive up the price and, to encourage sales, hand items through the crowd. When Greg's Damascus steel necklace, a beautiful circular collar that hooked onto itself, came up for bid, the commander wouldn't let it pass through the crowd; he didn't even have much to say about it.

"Why doesn't he pass it around?" I hissed to Greg. "He's holding onto it. It won't bring the price it ought to."

But Greg merely watched. He dreaded some comment from me, I suppose, that would bring him attention.

There was just one bid from the floor, and no follow-ups, and the commander lost interest. There was a lull. Greg's work hadn't received the bids it deserved. In the din of my own thoughts I missed the sale. The necklace disappeared without fanfare, and up went the next item, and out it went into the crowd.

"What'll you gimme, lemme hear a twenty, twenty, I've got

twenty, twenty, twenty, who'll gimme twenty-five . . ."

"How much did your necklace go for?" I whispered to Greg.

"Fifteen dollars."

I was offended. "It's worth a lot more."

"It went for a good cause."

"They're all going for a good cause," I retorted.

"Have you seen who's wearing it?" Greg pointed to a tall woman who leaned against the far wall of the shop. Gleaming against her dark sweater was the steel necklace.

"I didn't hear her buy it."

"She didn't. He bought it for her." Greg nodded his head toward the commander. "He gave it to his wife."

I was silenced. Everybody had known.

"The guy's our president. He works hard year around for the association. We saved him a buck or two. It was the least we could do." Greg smiled at me—laughed at me, actually—and ruffled my hair. "The girl who needs explanations." I rolled my eyes, embarrassed yet pleased to be corrected.

29

ALL NEXT DAY I heard the gong of hammer on iron repeating over and over: different tones, different rhythms. I entertained myself by making up melodies in the key struck.

The creek behind the farmhouse was different from the ditches and sloughs west of the mountains. Here the water ran fast and clear; there was no welter of muddy logs, standing water, or rotting cedar stumps exposed when, farther west in the watery part of the state, berry bushes and alders lose their leaves.

I followed the creek, climbed over a straight fence—no decay trapped in this dry wood—and hiked through the adjoining meadow. The wind blew from horizon to horizon and as I walked, the ground lifted and tipped toward the sky. The hammers flung up memories and the wind blew them to me whole. Summers in Kansas. Harvest. Mother and I collecting eggs. Grandpa's blacksmith shed. The whine of the grinding wheel as he sharpened his knives. Sweat running down the backs of my knees. Large, moist flies in the kitchen.

Almost as soon as Mother and Grandma and Grandpa and the barnyard and kitchen garden and cattle trough and chicken coop came as large as life to me, they slowly went away again, and I heard my own steps in the field. My childhood brushed against me and was gone.

Later, the winter sun shot its last shaft of light across the upper meadow, it shone through the tent and made a blue nylon cathedral in the cold air. I heard Greg approach. He unzipped the door, bent, and stepped inside.

"Have you been here all day?" he asked, crouching beside me where I lay in the sleeping bag. His breath wisped and vaporized.

"I took a long walk," I said. "This country reminds me of the Midwest."

He stretched out beside me on top of the goosedown.

"How's the smith?" I pulled my arms out of the sleeping bag and lifted myself onto one elbow. I smiled into his eyes.

"Just great." He took a deep, slow breath. "There's some fine ironwork going on."

I pushed the dark, springy hair back from his forehead and watched the curls cluster again. "Have you had time to do any work of your own?"

He shook his head. "Watched the demonstrator. Went to a board meeting. These weekends are for the general membership. I do my best work at home."

He kissed me slowly on my face, eyes, ears, collarbone; anything outside the sleeping bag. And then he was inside the sleeping bag with me, and this was our second time making love together. In place of shyness and eagerness to please, there was a slower rhythm between us. I knew his skin and hair now, his legs and feet. I was acquainted with his thighs and the bushing life between them. I remembered the way we'd talked and held each other in the truck coming over the mountain, and I moved against him until he would have no more playing and drove home in me, tense, then gave himself up, and later, sleepily, played with me until I could not be played with anymore, and I urged his hands and hurried and urged until Greg was erect once more and we were thrown into the heat all over again.

30

THE NEARER WE GOT to Hilliard the quieter Greg became.

"Hilliard's a world away from Eastern Washington," I said.

"Sure is."

"It would be nice to stay longer than just a weekend."

"You can say that again."

"I like winter camping."

"Good."

I settled back in my seat and mentally ran through a Bach fugue.

"I was going to stop by my mom's for a minute," he said.

"Fine."

"You don't have to come in."

"All right."

"I just have to talk to her for a minute," he said. "Anyway, you may not want to see her."

"Not yet."

"What about your piano lessons?"

"Oh, I still want to study with her."

"It wasn't a bad fight then?"

"No."

"It's none of my business."

"Right."

He slowed for a truck hauling hay.

"I made a decision this weekend," he said.

"It sounds serious."

"It is."

I waited.

"I'm going to say no to my mom."

"It *is* serious."

"Hardest thing in the world to do."

"She has a certain presence," I said. "Commanding."

"Absolutely."

"May I ask what you're going to say no to?"

"A project of hers. A business deal she wants me to help her with. If I'm going to stay in Hilliard I have to say no," he argued. "Can't just pick up and leave the country if I want to make a life here."

"You're all set in Hilliard," I agreed. "With your ironwork and teaching position, your name will mean something. Your shop will mean something. People will give you custom orders."

"They've already started."

"There you are."

"That's why I've got to say no."

"Absolutely." I waited. "Aren't you going to tell me about this business deal?"

"No."

"God, Greg, you build me up to this high pitch, and now you won't tell me."

"I can't. I just wanted you to know about my decision. I thought it would interest you." He shrugged. "You may have to say no to her, too, some day."

"When that day arrives I'll tell you about it," I said sardonically. "But not the specifics. Not the parts you'd really like to hear." I tried to guess. Something about the lawsuit, maybe. Perhaps she'd asked Greg to lie for her. But that wouldn't explain leaving the country. "You can't talk about it because she could get in trouble." His profile remained impassive. "But I can talk about it and you don't have to confirm or deny anything." No response. "She's going to buy bromeliads in Guatemala and sell them in the U.S. Sneak them across the border."

"What are bromeliads?"

"Plants. Highly specialized plants. They live on air, I think." No reaction. "Or something else illegal. Drugs."

"You can talk all day," he said. I settled back in the seat. Fierce, talented, independent, rude, venal Twilah. I didn't care what she did. I would continue to pay for two weekly lessons and work my heart out. Greg could tell me or not tell me about Guatemala, just as he wished, it didn't affect the music. I looked out the window. Soft rain, dripping firs, mulch of dead red alder leaves: I was happy to be back in western Washington. But Greg sat tense and silent behind the wheel, his pleasure from the weekend gone.

We stopped at Cedar Forge. He slid open the shop door and came back for the tent and camping gear. We stowed it in the locker at one end of the cold room. He walked over to his power hammer as if to greet an old friend he hadn't seen in a while.

"You're making a good life," I said, following him. "It holds together."

"I've achieved something." I wondered if he'd paid for his property and equipment himself or if his mother had helped. Not likely, to judge by that cheap bid of hers at the folk arts festival. We walked back to the locker. I tucked in the strap to the canteen so it wouldn't catch in the door.

"How long are you going to be in Hilliard?" he said.

"I have to be back in Seattle by the boys' birthdays," I answered. "I promised."

"You're going to stay there?"

"My job's in Seattle." We walked outside. Greg slid the shop door shut and padlocked it. I tried to lighten the mood. "Now that you're building a trade, making your reputation, saying no to your mom, you expect me to know what I'm doing, too."

"Damn right." He led off to the truck and we drove into town.

"I thought you were going to stop at your mom's," I said. Either he'd forgotten or half-changed his mind, because he stopped, made a U-turn, and went back. He parked in front of her apartment house.

"I'll just be a minute," he said.

He took the curb and parking strip in two strides, jogged up the walk, landed on the old porch, and disappeared into the house. I bent to look up at the second-story window, doubting I'd ever be invited there again. I straightened and sat tall. If Twilah looked out the window, she'd see only my coat through the windshield. Maybe she wouldn't recognize me. Maybe she wouldn't associate me with the day her son said *no*.

Greg stayed in the house longer than he said he would. When he finally came down the sidewalk, his face was dark. Twilah had followed him downstairs and now she stood in the doorway, wearing a long, purple dressing gown. I resisted the impulse to duck. She couldn't miss seeing me now. I waved, but she didn't wave back. We drove to the docks in silence: Greg had forgotten to drop me at the old hotel. He turned off the engine and held the keys in his hand.

He hit the steering wheel. "I said no." He sat in moody silence. "She always gets around me."

I sat in his silence; in the powerlessness he felt when he was with her. Here at the boat basin the windshield was misting over.

"I'll walk home," I finally said, unwilling to discuss his mother and perhaps end up in another argument. "I need to stretch."

He roused. "Do you mind?"

"I don't mind. I'd like it."

"I'll bring your pack over later."

"Okay."

I left him sitting in the truck, and walked toward the cannery. I stopped once in the street and looked down at the dock. Masts and boat shrouds made a continuous V, the dock their center. Creosoted pilings fell away into the distance, growing smaller as the perspective lengthened. Visually, I added the shrouds to the pilings and saw a new set of shapes.

First drops of rain wet my face and dimpled the standing water in front of the cannery. It was almost twilight. Gulls circled and squealed. A heron landed on the dock below me, cautious and leggy. Its size startled me: bigger than a dog. I turned away from the channel and set off for my rooms. The street ahead, silver in the mist, went away from me in a slow, uphill curve.

"Virginia!" Greg was waving from the truck. "It's raining!" He motioned for me to come back, but I hesitated.

"Come to the boat!" I walked back and followed him down the ramp. The heron squawked and lifted, looking like a bag of feathers before it straightened out in graceful flight. Now that I was on the same level with them, riggings and masts seemed to lean the other way, toward a center instead of away. With automated hiccups, bilge pumps turned themselves on and off, busily emptying rainwater from boats. At the commercial fishing moorage a radio blasted rock music. Even in the rain the fishermen were out working on their lines.

We reached THUNDER. Greg threw his pack in the cockpit and climbed down into the cabin. I followed and watched him make a fire in the woodburner. His mother and the business deal weighed heavily in the silence. He wanted me there, but evidently not for talk. I had just about decided to leave and make a fire in my own stove, turn the heat on in my own rooms, when he took me by the hand and led me into the fo'c's'le. We lay on the wide berth and made love. No laughing. No ecstatic moans. Just a guttural now and then. For a while I had the ragged feeling that this sex was a painkiller to make him feel better, but, carried by the weight of his emotion, I went with him to a dark, private place where I was exposed to something rough and masculine. Perhaps I was taken there to help light the space.

When we emerged together on deck, it was night, and the wind was blowing. Halyards banged. I watched Greg check the lines. Even in the wet wind he seemed to me to be working at a forge, transforming steel to hot iron, moody anger to heat and love and back again to moody anger.

31

SINCE I WANTED TO LEARN PIANO and Twilah wanted to teach piano, we resumed the lessons as if nothing had happened.

"There's a competition coming up in the three-counties area," Twilah said one Tuesday at the conclusion of a lesson. "Would you like to enter?"

"When is it?"

"April 21st."

"I'll be gone by then," I said. "I'll be back in Seattle."

"If you are studying with me," Twilah said firmly, "you're eligible, no matter where you live."

"I'll think about it," I said.

"There's a prize."

"What is it?"

"Three-hundred dollars and a weekly lesson at Western State University for one semester."

"They'll all be young performers."

"That's got nothing to do with it!" When Twilah felt fierce, the skin around her nose tightened and turned white; as it did then. "Never say you're too old to do a thing! Age has nothing to do with anything. Anyway," she added illogically, "you're only thirty-four. You'll play Beethoven. You're well-suited to Beethoven. A movement from one of the sonatas, I would think."

"How long do I play?"

"Up to fifteen minutes."

"Are there many contestants?"

"Usually about twenty. It's an all-day affair."

I saw myself sitting in a row of pinafored girls, a grown woman in a children's recital.

"Is there an age limit?" I asked.

"You fall under it!" Twilah snapped. "And as to a lower limit, you fall above it. So you see, you're safe." She wrote in my assignment book and stood to leave.

"I'll walk you to town," I said, unwilling to end the lesson. "I'm going that way."

"In general, you can take the adagio sections more slowly," she said as we left the lower end of High Street and began climbing toward the restaurants and shops. "You're too impatient with the tempo—" She was about to say more when she stopped abruptly. "Heather!"

Heather Desmond emerged from My Favorite Things Boutique carrying a gold dress box. She extended a many-braceleted arm toward Twilah.

"How are you? I was just thinking of you!"

"Wonderful to see you," Twilah responded in a voice I didn't know.

After Heather had turned the conversation to the hospital auxilliary's upcoming luncheon at which her husband, the administrator, would be guest of honor, she said, "You're out shopping?"

"Teaching," Twilah said.

"At the—hotel? Marguerite Cleary's apartment?" Heather's eyes grazed mine, as if faintly remembering someone who had once played background music for her Christmas party.

"I'm subletting," I said, as if to introduce myself.

"There's a piano on the second floor," Twilah said almost apologetically. "I give her a lesson twice a week."

Heather looked down at her wristwatch. "Heavens!" she exclaimed, adjusting the narrow gold band. "It's time for me to pick up the children from school. Sorry to dash. So good to see you."

She shifted the dress box to the other arm. "So we can count on you for the luncheon, Twilah?"

"By all means. Lovely seeing you."

"That woman ignores me," I said as Heather half-ran toward her car. "I think she's suspicious of my address."

Twilah shrugged. "Heather Desmond is a limited woman."

"Why bother with her?"

"If I refused to bother with limited people," Twilah said testily, "I'd be alone most of the time."

"How does Heather know Marguerite Cleary?" I asked after we'd walked another half-block.

"Everyone in Hilliard knows everyone else in Hilliard. Even you, it seems, and you've only been here since November." She turned to look at me. "How *do* you know Marguerite Cleary, and what is your great interest in her?"

"I don't know her," I said, "but I've seen the name written in her books." I decided to be truthful. "I saw a legal transcript with her name in the caption."

Twilah frowned.

"What's more, I read it."

"A lawsuit should come as no surprise to *you*," she said. "You make your money off the nasty things."

God, she's unpleasant, I thought. Maybe it's time to go back to Seattle. Lots of great piano teachers there. Probably twenty Twilahs. Yes, I'll go back to Seattle. Find a teacher who stands above the landscape, but is pleasant.

"Someone has to file the nasty thing before it's a lawsuit," I pointed out.

"In any case," she said, "Marguerite Cleary won't be back. She's gone. It's the convalescent home we're after." I caught the lift of her chin; the bright eye. "It's a well-known fact the home is below-standard. It's time someone did something."

She didn't say it but I could read the message in her eyes: Mind your own business. The trouble was, I didn't really have any business of my own.

32

Immersed in hours of piano practice, I saw almost no one. Greg called less frequently, and I didn't want to see Mr. Raithel or the tired waitress or anyone on the streets of Hilliard. Twilah was different. She was permanent. A building. A boulder. You might run into a building or a boulder and hurt yourself, but it never occurred to you to want the boulder somewhere else. It was there.

Straddling two lives again, I picked up Lawrence and Matthew before dinner on a Wednesday. Ron said they were finishing up a television show and would I like to come in and have a cup of tea?

I didn't see Anna anywhere around. We watched the end of a science program called Curiosity. This was the first time since the divorce I'd sat in the same room with the three of them. The pattern of the cup I drank from was as blue and white as ever; the TV was louder, the boys were taller, but the room was the same. It felt like what it was: a past home, a memory I could rely on. Later, as the boys and I prepared to leave, I thanked Ron for the tea. But the boys looked wary and Ron grew distant again and eager for us to go. Hello's and good-bye's were still hard. I tried to kick into higher gear by remembering the way I'd felt in the TV room, the cup of tea between my hands, my sons and their father nearby. But in the dark and cold of the porch, with a breeze softly moaning, I caught the downward spiral of my feelings, Ron's feelings, and, I think, Matt and Lawrence's feelings, although they were making a big deal of running to the car; trying to get through the gate first, arguing over front seat/back seat.

Most of my conversation with them these days, it seemed, was in cars, restaurants, and movie theatres. Transitory places. But soon I would be back in my Seattle house, and they would stay with me on Wednesday nights and alternate weekends, the way they used to. We would chat in the kitchen. I'd give them backrubs before they fell asleep. Call them in to dinner when the light faded and cook oatmeal for them while the sound of the morning news flowed around us.

That evening on the way to dinner they told me about school. They'd taken a field trip to Boeing Aircraft and seen the biggest hangar in the world. The gym teacher made them do calisthenics and the kids called him Chief of Police behind his back. I detected respect.

Later, in a movie theatre during slow scenes, they rested their heads on my shoulders, one to the left, one to the right. I laid my cheek against one boy, then the other.

Is this the horror of separation from the children? I wondered as I drove north toward Hilliard in the dark. Is this as bad as it gets? Loss, yes. Sadness and guilt, definitely. Yet none of us has fallen apart. The bonds are strong. Loosened but strong.

A sideways-blowing mist passed in front of my headlights like a cloud of salt across the highway. I turned on the heater and drove along I-5 toward the border with Canada, toward the pocket of the Sound where winds reach all the way from Japan. I made up a story about a woman who was strong enough to find her own work and do it alone, if necessary; who could fill her own studio; who didn't return to her old home, the past. A woman whose children didn't need her to be there on a daily basis anymore.

33

Although winter was still going strong in mid February, boaters were beginning to arrive from Seattle and Arlington, Marysville and Vernon, even from Yakima and as far east as Idaho to check on their boats, unroll the sails, scrub down the fiberglass. A few, like Greg, had beautiful wooden boats, modest or grand, with decks to paint and bright work to polish. A wooden boat farther down the dock from THUNDER was for sale, wrapped in plastic sheeting, a bad move, Greg said, because the boat couldn't breathe.

"Boats breathe?" I said.

"Certainly. You've got to let a thing breathe, especially in salt air; not try to preserve it under plastic."

The boat owners in Hilliard were mostly commercial fishermen who kept up their own rough but costly vessels docked across the harbor from the pleasure craft. Year-round, sailboats and yachts were maintained by locals who took it easy through the winter, answering calls for batteries or emergency bilge pumps in their own good time—"Something in the marine air makes them casual about work," Greg said—until spring brought them rushing to the marina to subsidize their winter sloth.

Ron called not long after I'd been back in Hilliard.

"Hello, Virginia." He sounded upset.

"Hello, Ron."

"Things have changed a little around here."

"Are the boys all right?"

"They're fine." Silence. He never called like this, out of the blue.

"When did you plan to be back to Seattle?" he asked.

"By the boys' birthdays."

"Could you make it sooner?"

"Has something happened?" I said.

He cleared his throat. "Anna and I decided to part company. I think the kids feel—uneasy."

I hadn't thought Matt and Lawrence were that close to the woman. Still, her presence must have filled in family for them: the mommy, daddy, and two kids all living under one roof. Judging from Ron's voice, it had filled in family for him, too.

"Wait. Here's Matthew," he said.

"Hi, Mom."

"How are you, son?"

"Good." Matthew was silent for a moment. Even at nine, his silences were dignified.

"My birthday's pretty soon," he said.

"March 20th."

"You said you'd be home by then."

"And I will. My renters are moving out on the 1st. I'll be there."

"Good," said Matt. Next, Lawrence.

"Hi, Mom."

"Hi, Lawrence."

"When are you coming back?" It was nice to have this welcoming committee.

"Soon," I said. "Shall I come down this Saturday?"

"Sure. I have a basketball game."

"Good."

"So does Matt."

"I'll watch them both."

"They're at the same time."

"Well . . . I'll watch half of each."

"Watch his half first and my half last," said Lawrence shrewdly. "We always come from behind."

Ron sounded better when he returned to the line. "So you'll be down Saturday?"

"Saturday. Regular time."

"See you then."

I put down the receiver. I was going to have to go home. Well, if not *home* since I didn't know exactly where *home* was, but at least to Seattle. I couldn't put off the call to Ross any longer. I dialed my old office. Tried to inject myself with humility. Twisted the telephone cord and sought the right tone of voice to ask for my job back.

"How's the country girl?" Ross said. He always called us girls. We were his. He liked to think he gave us our commissions, while I thought of it as paying *him* a commission. It was a difference in viewpoint that annoyed him and made me just the slightest bit uncontrollable, a kind of subversive.

"I'm fine," I said cheerfully. "Ready to come back to work." Judging by his silence, my tone of voice was off. The humility felt off, too.

"What do you *mean*, you're ready to come back?" Ross said.

"My leave of absence," I said. "The three months are almost up."

He hesitated. Must be playing a game with me, I thought, he doesn't want to appear too eager. Resents my long vacation.

"Actually, Virginia," he said lightly, "the staff is balanced just about right. A new girl came on board."

"Oh." There was a silence, but he said nothing more. "You don't need me?"

"Not at the moment. But you know how this business is. Down today, up tomorrow."

"But Ross," I said, trying to control the shake in my voice. The effort must have gratified him. "I thought I still had my job. We talked about it before I left."

"I don't remember any guarantees, Virginia. I needed more staff, I got them, and now I'm obligated to keep them busy."

I wanted to lose my temper and say something memorable. But I might need Ross again some day. "Let me know when you want a good reporter," I said stiffly.

"Where can you be reached?"

"After March 1st, same number. Same house in Seattle." I gave him my Hilliard number just in case someone quit, and said goodbye.

No job, and my money running out. I'd have to call another freelance firm in the city. But when I called several other agencies, they said they were already overstaffed. Jobs were down.

I left my Hilliard number. "Will you call if you need someone for overflow?"

"This isn't a Seattle number, is it?" they asked.

"No. You can reach me in Hilliard." I felt their interest decline. "Call collect," I added.

Following an impulse, I looked at the transcript of Twilah's deposition and called the reporting firm listed on the cover.

"Why, yes," said the owner, Ms. Liknel. "I could use you. One of my reporters just had a baby. She's taking a leave of absence."

Ah, yes. The leave of absence.

"Tell me about yourself," she said.

I did.

"We aren't as busy as the reporters in Seattle, you know," she warned. "And our page rates are lower." She explained that her clients were strung out between Bellingham and Vernon and, to the west, the islands. "We fly or take the ferry to Friday Harbor," she said.

I made an appointment to meet her. But within the hour she called back to say a job had come in and she needed me the next day. I jumped in the car and made a fast trip to Seattle for my steno machine. I felt as if I hadn't written shorthand in years.

Still, I hadn't forgotten. The job went well. The plaintiffs, homeowners, claimed the defendant contractor owed them money because he'd put in a cement patio when the plans called for brick. Twenty-five pages. Small potatoes. Up here, I realized, away from the city, there would be no lucrative corporate lawsuits.

34

THE DEPOSITION ALMOST MADE ME LATE for my piano lesson and I arrived at my rooms only ten minutes ahead of Twilah.

"I haven't practiced!" I wailed. "I worked today. I have to start reporting again, Twilah. I don't see how I can find time for lessons, much less enter the piano competition. Everything's different now. Everything's changed."

She took off her coat, hung it on the hook behind the kitchen door, and said, "Make us a cup of tea."

I pushed my machine and briefcase out of the way and filled the kettle with water. The sun on the channel behind me may have been beautiful, and probably was, but I no longer had time for the luxuries. I ran the water hard until it backed up and flowed out the spout, then slung the kettle onto the burner.

"I haven't even thought about Beethoven," I said. "I haven't practiced scales since day before yesterday. I'm not prepared at all for a lesson."

"We're never prepared," Twilah said. "We simply have to pretend that we are."

"I've always been prepared," I said. "Maybe you don't know how hard I've worked these last few months."

"I think I know."

"Arranged my whole life around piano lessons," I said. "There was no pretense about it."

As soon as the water boiled we carried the cups and teapot to the music room. "I prepared myself thoroughly for coming to

Hilliard," I continued. "Rented out my house. Lived on savings. Drove to see my kids. I thought I had a job to come back to." I set the tray on the piano and turned on the heater. "Believe me, all this has been no accident, Twilah." I sat down hard on the straight chair and opened Beethoven.

"Just shut up and start playing," she said. I recoiled. But I played, and it was awful. I lost my place and botched the fingering.

"You see? I have no margin of safety. No resilience. If I don't have time for calm practice, I can't play at all. There is no way I'm going to enter that competition."

"Balderdash," she said. With no sympathy or agreement to provide me with an escape route, there was nothing to do but play. Things began to smooth out.

"See? You can play even when things aren't perfect," Twilah said at the end of the first movement. "In fact, playing will help make things perfect."

I shook back my hair. "I'm going to have to fit music into my life from now on," I said, "instead of fitting my life around music. I don't have the luxury anymore. And it happened with almost no warning. I wasn't ready for this, Twilah."

"We never are," she said. "But there's no doubt in my mind you can manage it. Sleep two hours less a night. Spend less."

"I have a mortgage and child support payments," I muttered. "I can't cut those."

"Are you getting any money from your ex-husband?"

"A monthly payment on the second trust deed." I ripped through a measure.

"When will he pay it off?"

"In twenty years." For once I could have said, "None of your business," but I didn't. "I'm satisfied," I said. "We made an agreement."

"Well, then, everything's going as planned. Play." I played. Not only did the fingering and phrasing improve, but I began to feel strong, even powerful, as if I had something to say back to Beethoven.

"Bravo!" Twilah said when I finished the second movement. "That shows what a little stress can do!"

We walked back along the smelly hallway. I felt wonderful.

"Are you still returning to Seattle?" she asked.

"I have to be back by the boys' birthdays."

"But if you're working up here—"

"I can't make enough money up here in the boonies. No offense. The money is in the city. That's where the litigation is, the big lawsuits. I'll get my old job back soon, you watch."

She shrugged. "I managed to stay alive up here," she said. "Greg and I managed to stay alive. I'll admit I traveled quite a bit to buy merchandise. And for years I played concerts five months out of the year. It was grueling. Fortunately, Arturo was always here." She got her coat down from the hook. "Even now . . . you have to keep working at it, Virginia." She thrust her long arms into the sleeves of her parka and stopped. Her black eyes locked onto mine. "Tomorrow is an important day. I don't mind telling you it could change Arturo's and my life."

I returned her bright gaze. "What's happening tomorrow?"

She slapped her right thigh. "We get compensated for our suffering. This hip." She was finally going to tell me. "The convalescent home neglected me and"—she spat out the name— "Marguerite Cleary neglected me. Everyone in town knows I was neglected. The hospital knows it, too. Morgan and Heather Desmond have seen it happen over and over again. Doctors on the hospital staff send patients to the home and they're neglected. Too many people are neglected, Virginia! I won't be neglected! I won't let Arturo be neglected! I won't let Gregory be neglected!"

My name was omitted. Her speech had built up to such force that there were no words left in the room. If I'd spoken, it would have been like interrupting an artist at work; like trying to stop a sexual climax when it's already started.

After she left I walked into the absent woman's studio. The shelves and everything on them looked pitiful. Dusty. Forgotten. No one to claim them. While I considered whether there would be enough money for me to hang on in the old hotel until Ross needed me again—*if* Ross needed me again—and what I could tell my children if I didn't find work in Seattle, I went to the cupboard under the kitchen sink and returned with the feather duster to lightly flick Marguerite's books and drawings and mementos. I began to feel better. Though the room was still someone else's, I no longer felt strange standing in it. I sat down in a straight chair. I had not given any thought to what kind of woman Marguerite Cleary was. I knew she was creative. I knew she was scared. I knew she'd been Greg's girl friend for a while. That was a long way from knowing *her*.

35

INTO MY DEEP SLEEP came a sound like a gunshot. Jerking as though hit, I sat up and squinted at the light coming from the studio. With one hand over my heart to keep it in place, I slipped out of bed. On bare feet, my back against the wall, I slid toward the bedroom door and craned my neck into the light. But the angle of sight was wrong. I couldn't see without being seen. Another shot. No, not a shot. A drawer slammed shut. Whoever it was thought they were alone.

"Damn!"

I drew back sharply, then inched my head into the light again. A tall, skinny woman stood on the far side of the studio rummaging through papers. Her red hair flowed loosely. I glimpsed beige cord pants, a pullover sweater, high-topped tennis shoes. Suddenly she crossed the studio in three strides until she stood in the hall outside my bedroom. She reached around the door jamb. I flattened myself against the wall and watched her broad, reddened hand feel for the light switch. The bedroom light snapped on. In one sweeping eye movement, she saw the slept-in bed and me. She sucked in a breath and stood motionless while I stared at her.

"Who are you?" she asked.

"Virginia Johnstone. I live here," I said. "Temporarily." Blue eyes blazed at me. "You're Marguerite Cleary."

She nodded and stepped back into the studio. "I didn't know they found a renter."

"I'm subletting," I said. I wanted to keep the terminology

straight. Although she looked younger than I, thirty, maybe, she seemed old somehow. The red hair hung long and glossy, like storybook hair, but her face had a used look. Struggle showed around the eyes. Behind her it seemed a wind had whipped through the studio. I glanced from litter pile to litter pile.

"It's a mess," she said. "I'm moving out." In two long steps she was back at the desk tossing photographs into a produce box: 'Golden Delicious, Yakima Valley Farms.' She shot more drawers back and forth on their runners and started a new box for books.

"This is a wonderful room," I said.

"Thanks."

"You have a lot of beautiful things."

"Yeah. I treasure them."

I couldn't go back to bed, not now that the absent woman was here.

"I'll try to be quiet so you can get some sleep."

"I'm not tired," I said. "Can I help?"

She shrugged. "Okay."

I set boxes on the landing. On the way back, I took down the blanket hanging between the living room and studio. It would just get in the way.

"I'm living here temporarily," I repeated.

"What do you do?"

"Take piano lessons."

She laughed. "In Hilliard?"

"In Hilliard." I shook out the blanket and folded it. I stood there in my flannel nightgown, feet getting cold on the pinewood floor.

"What's your line of work?" she asked.

"Court reporter."

"I was in the courthouse today." She worked a thumb tack out of the bulletin board.

"I see."

"I came back to straighten out some legal affairs."

"Did you get them taken care of?"

"Oh, yes. I sure did."

I wanted to ask what happened, to babble about Twilah and the convalescent home, the lawsuit, the deposition I'd read, my old home, my temporary home, my mother, women who leave, women who come back, studios that are alternately filled, stripped, filled, stripped.

"I used your wood in the stove," I said. "I found it under the steps outside."

"Yeah, I split that wood." She stopped to appraise me. "Can you help carry these boxes down to my van?"

"Yes. You can sleep on the sofa. It's your sofa."

"Not mine. It was here." She worked for a while without talking. When she bent, her shining hair swung above the boxes. "So you didn't hear me come in, huh?"

"I didn't think you'd be back."

She stopped working. "Why did you think that?"

I placed one cold foot on top of the other. "I called this room 'the absent woman's studio.'"

"Well, I'm not absent, not with all my stuff here." She flung her arm out. "I made all this. I don't like to be called absent when my stuff's still here." She looked at me closely. "See my work? See my things?"

"I see them." I was afraid of her eye contact, her confidence, her creativity, her anger. She reminded me of Twilah. They were two of a kind.

"People want you absent so they can blame you for things," she said, "but they want you present to empty the bedpans."

I changed position and put the cold foot on top of the warmer one.

"Someone brought a lawsuit against the convalescent home where I worked," she said. "I told them I'd be back to testify. I told my landlord I'd be back. I left all my stuff, sort of collateral.

I guess everyone thought it was junk."

"It's not junk."

"I make things. I leave them here. If they think it's junk, that's their problem."

"Why did you leave?"

"To get some money."

"Did you get it?"

"I sure did. I earned it. Not the pitiful wages they pay at the convalescent home, either. And I got a lawyer just in case I need one." She lifted her chin defiantly. "Which I don't."

I watched her slip a rubberband around some paintbrushes. Her sharp elbows almost stuck through her sweater. She had a high, rounded, dainty forehead, like a Dutch portrait, perhaps Vermeer's young woman bent over lacework. But she wasn't bent over lacework. She was moving about the studio, almost twitching with nervous energy. She dropped the paintbrushes into a box.

"I'm glad you came back," I said. "I wondered who you were."

"I came back for my stuff and to settle the legal thing. After that, I'm outta here." She folded her thin arms across her chest, narrowed her eyes, and looked at me closely. "They're all bastards."

"Who?"

She shrugged. "It doesn't matter now. It's over."

"Has the case been dismissed?"

"Yeah," she said. "No negligence. The judge himself said there's no evidence. No case. Dismissed."

I dropped the blanket and stood on it to warm my feet. She stopped packing and squatted on the floor with a small sketch pad and pencil.

"I worked in the home," she said, drawing an idle line. Her hair hid her face. "A patient rolled out of bed on purpose when the railing was down. Tried to say it was my fault." She turned the line into a hospital bed. "I was standing right there giving a bath." She stabbed the paper with the pencil point. "I never leave patients alone with the bed rail down." She scribbled some more lines that turned into a hospital bed in disarray.

"The rail . . ."

Marguerite drew an overlarge lever that could have been a box, a shoe, a banana, a trowel. The main thing was its prominence. "She knew where it was. She reached for it and she found it." Marguerite threw down the pencil.

"Why would anyone do a thing like that?" It was beyond belief.

"Mean," she said. "And bored. I think she laid there and planned the whole thing. For money. A lawsuit." Marguerite Cleary rose easily, almost gracefully, to a standing position. "Malpractice. Negligence." She returned to the desk, pulled out a drawer full of papers, and shook it upside down above a box. "So how did you end up in the old hotel?"

"An ad in the paper," I said. "And your red curtains. I'm not an old-hotel type of person," I continued. "In fact, coming to Hilliard was sort of a strange thing for me to do. I came up almost on a whim. It wasn't a practical move. It was quite impractical, as a matter of fact. But I've been happy here."

I hadn't ever said that, either to myself or anyone else. I'd been happy here.

"I was happy here, too," said Marguerite, "until the lawsuit."

"When did you come to Hilliard?"

"Several years ago. Came out from Kansas with a boyfriend. Broke up with him and stayed on. Wanted to get away from my family for a while. Big family, little town. Wanted to try my wings." She squatted again and began rummaging through papers on the bottom shelf of the bookcase. Her shoulder blades were sharp ridges under her sweater, yet she gave the impression of strength. As if, thin and delicate and tall, she could still fly by herself, and still resist the forces ranged against her. She twisted her head and looked up at me. "But family is the first place I went when I was in trouble. Isn't that interesting? I worked for my dad on the farm and got some money together. Got some muscle, too." She clamped one hand around her skinny upper arm and flexed a bicep. "Thin but wiry," she said. She rotated her neck to the right, to the left, then walked over to the window. When she pulled back the curtain, the floodlight in the shipyard gave a stagey look to the night. "They've almost finished another boat."

"That's a pretty risky thing to do, roll out of bed on purpose," I said.

"Well, this was no ordinary lady."

"That lady is my piano teacher," I blurted out. "The best piano teacher I've ever had."

Marguerite Cleary shrugged.

"She never would talk to me about the lawsuit," I said. "I wanted her to."

"That's because she's ashamed of herself." Such an old-fashioned expression, and I didn't expect a young woman to use it: maybe that's the way people still talked in Kansas.

"I've only known her since November," I added. "She stays sort of aloof. We're not what you'd call friends."

"And you won't be, either, unless you come into some money or win the Nobel prize."

"You think she's a snob?"

"I thought she was my friend. I knew her son. But I guess I wasn't good enough for either of them." She snorted. "She's a broken-down piano teacher in a broken-down town. No offense."

"None taken." I didn't ask her about Greg. I really didn't want to know. "Tomorrow I'll help you carry boxes downstairs."

"I'll sleep on the couch tonight," she said, "what's left of it." I didn't know if she meant the couch or the night. "I've got blankets in my van."

"Do you want the specimens on the stairsteps?" I asked.

"Nah. I can always find more."

"No starfish in Kansas."

"Dried flowers," she said. "Dried wheat, and grasses, too. Everyone dries sunflowers, but you don't see their dried seed heads very often. I brought tumbleweed into my folks' house. We put colored lights on it for Christmas. I make pheasant feather wreaths. You have to go with what you find."

I lay awake and tried to picture an old woman throwing herself onto the floor for money. I easily imagined Twilah in a hospital bed, her face drawn and pale, her straggling hair in need of a shampoo. I saw a bedside table, plastic pitcher of water, tray with used breakfast dishes that hadn't been picked up yet. But I couldn't imagine her hand creeping out from under the bedclothes, reaching through the bars of the guard rail for a lever . . .

I couldn't bear to imagine the empty bed with Twilah lying helpless on the floor beside it.

36

Twilah called to cancel our next lesson. "Something's come up," she said in a taut voice. "By the way, the audition is this Saturday."

"What audition?"

"Audition for the piano competition."

"You didn't tell me there was an audition."

"Well, it's just a formality. You'll have no difficulty being accepted."

"Why didn't you tell me?"

"You would have just worried. You're ready. Don't think about it."

"But what will I play?"

"The same sonata you'll play at the competition. Believe me, Virginia, it's a mere formality. It's barely worth mentioning."

"I noticed you didn't mention it," I said. "What time shall I pick you up?"

"Eight-thirty Saturday morning. I'll be waiting." There was no hint that she had been embarrassed or overturned in a court proceeding earlier. Only this new, tight voice, this clipped quality to the conversation; it was not a conversation, really, but more like an exchange of signals.

I invited Greg for dinner, but extracting information from him was no easier.

"Marguerite Cleary was here yesterday," I said nonchalantly. "She got her things."

He leaned against the kitchen counter, his hands in his pockets. "I heard she was in town."

"Did you see her?"

"No."

"The studio's empty," I said. "It looks so strange." He didn't respond. "I know how to fill it," I said, "but I need your help."

"What do you have in mind?"

"Help me move the piano."

"Does it have wheels?"

"Sure does."

The old upright was hard to get in motion, but once rolling it traveled easily down the hall, through the kitchen and living room, and into the studio where our voices bounced off the bare walls and ceiling.

"Is this where you want it?" he asked doubtfully. We'd rolled it to the center of the room.

"Until I decide how to arrange things."

"It doesn't look like there's much to arrange." He glanced around at the empty space. "We'll call it Virginia's studio now," he said, and smiled for the first time that evening. He almost seemed pleased with himself, as if moving the piano had been his idea. "The court case is over," he said.

I put my arms around him, kissed him, and waited for an embrace that didn't come. I dropped my arms. "Marguerite Cleary told me," I said. "I didn't know whether to believe her or not."

"You can believe her." He went around to the keyboard and picked at a few notes. "Mom's stunned. So am I." He attempted 'Chopsticks' then stepped back from the piano, walked to the window and back to the piano again. "The lawsuit was a bad idea. Her lawyer should never have let her go through with it." He started toward the kitchen and I followed him. The chicken I'd put on the stove late in the afternoon smelled of onion, oregano and tomatoes. I wasn't hungry; I didn't think Greg was, either.

"What happened in court?" I asked.

He sat down at the table. "I don't want to talk about it." A little later he asked, "Didn't Marguerite tell you what happened?"

"She told me her side of it."

"That's the only side that matters now." Greg wasn't going to elaborate. This much I knew: his mother had been humiliated, and, indirectly, so had he. Although there had been only a motion to dismiss, no jury to see it, still, it had been a public judgment, an official humiliation. The newspaper would report it. And he'd lost a girl friend over it. I put one elbow on the table and leaned my chin in my hand.

"It's none of my business," I said. He looked up and I smiled. He smiled back, a rueful half smile. I served up two plates of chicken and we plodded through dinner.

37

Twilah was unusually quiet on Saturday morning. We drove north along Chuckanut Drive, a road hacked out of steep cliffs overlooking Bellingham Bay. On our left, wind whipped the blue water into low whitecaps. Popcorn, Greg would call it. Two sailboats tacked with the wind, their white canvas sails bellying. On the right, boulders and cliff wall held back tons of earth from the highway, and gnarled trees and brittle little bushes straggled up out of stone, life looking for a toehold. The road led away from the cliff, away from the bay, through a thick grove of trees. We crossed a narrow bridge and took a sharp turn. The creek beneath us, dark and cool, took its turn, too.

"I'm not nervous for this audition," I finally said just outside Bellingham.

"It's a mere formality."

"It's good to be riding with you in this—majestic scenery," I said. I tried to loosen up. "There's so much to experience," I went on. "Even learning the simplest thing, doing it well, like being a fern or a giant spruce or a dry little bush in a rock, seems profound."

"Just drive."

When we reached the University I located the visitors' parking lot. Though I didn't actually escort her to the music department—she pointed the building out to me—I felt Twilah depending on my energy to get her there. We took seats in the back row. Young pianists, teachers, and parents sat in small groups dispersed through the half-empty auditorium listening to a boy play Brahms. Twilah didn't join in the scattered applause when he got up from the piano, and she barely seemed present. I experienced a moment of panic and nausea. *Oh, Twilah*, I wanted to say, *why am I here with these children?* But I had to answer my own question: *Play, Virginia. If you can't be a giant spruce, be—a fern.*

A judge called my name. The walk up the aisle was long. I felt young pianists—my competitors—and their parents watching me.

Thirty-four is so old, I thought.

The piano bench scraped against the stage floor when I moved it back from the keyboard.

"Take a moment to acquaint yourself with the action," said a man's voice from somewhere in the hall. I played a scale and an arpeggio. It was a lovely piano. The action was more solid than the rinky-tink piano in the hotel, and the tone was lush. I played a soft chord and a loud chord. Definitely more variation in loud and soft than I was used to. I wished I could play on this piano every day.

I began Beethoven. My hands were damp. One finger slipped off a black key. I passed through the first few measures, stopped thinking about my hands and entered the piece. The music that came out of the piano sounded firm and rich to me. Better than at the old hotel. Better than in Seattle. I muddied a phrase and concentrated harder. Then I lost myself in the music. Before I was ready to stop, it was over; the sonata movement had never seemed shorter. I pushed back the bench, stood up, descended the stage steps, and took the long aisle back to Twilah.

When I was even with the judges' seats, one of them spoke. "Thank you for coming today. We'll contact Mrs. Chan sometime this week." I nodded and kept walking.

Outside in the sunshine I didn't need to ask how I'd played.

"Never better," Twilah said cryptically. I smiled. Gaps in memory, the fumbled notes which I'd dreaded, which I'd expected, hadn't materialized. On stage, music flowed out of me. I looked sideways at my teacher.

"It's because of you," I said, but she didn't seem to hear. She was barely keeping up so I slowed and we strolled through campus toward the parking lot. The school buildings turned their warm brick-and-masonry faces toward me.

"I wish I'd finished college."

At that, Twilah looked up, but without the usual weight and force and fire of her opinion. I wanted to ask her about her conservatory training, but the way she carried her head, the way she looked at one spot in front of her, remote, withdrawn, silenced me. We drove back along the Chuckanut, down into the flat farmland, and home to the edge of the Sound.

"Thank you for making the audition possible," I said as she opened the car door in front of her apartment house. "I've never had a teacher I worked so hard for. I wish—I wish I'd known you much earlier in my life." My throat thickened with emotion. I wasn't sure she heard me: certainly, she didn't acknowledge my little speech.

38

I'D INVITED GREG for dinner again, but he called ahead.

"Go ahead and eat without me," he said. "Arturo and I are talking. It's hard to break off."

By the time he finally came to my rooms, it was nine-thirty. He hung his coat on the hook behind the door and glanced at me as if he didn't quite see me. He looked pale and tired. I didn't question him about the late hour.

"Have you eaten?"

"With Arturo," he said.

"Arturo and your mom?"

He shook his head. "Just Arturo." We'd reached the living room and he sank onto the sofa. "Mom's had a breakdown."

"Breakdown?" I heard the word but couldn't connect it to Twilah. "You mean . . ." He leaned his head back on the sofa and closed his eyes. I perched on the edge beside him. "Where is she?"

"At home. Let's be still for a while," he said. "No talking."

I went to the kitchen, poured us both a drink, and stood at the counter staring blankly into a Scotch and water. When I returned, Greg still had his head back on the couch, eyes closed. I sat down beside him, holding the two glasses. Finally I drank out of one.

"Virginia?"

"I'm here. I made us drinks."

He opened his eyes. "What time is it?"

"After ten. Want to sleep over?" When we slept together it was usually in his boat. My bed was narrow.

"Yes," he said. He drank a little Scotch and handed the glass back to me, then bent to unlace his shoes. I began rubbing his back, up and down, side to side. His shoulders were knotted.

"Can you hear the phone from the bedroom?" he asked.

"It has a long cord," I said. "I'll bring it into the studio. We can hear it from there."

"Virginia's studio," he said, and turned his head to give me a wan smile. We went to bed immediately. Bent against Greg, back to front, two spoons, I lay awake thinking of Twilah. That my strong, talented teacher could even dream of injuring herself had frightened me. And now a breakdown.

Greg moaned lightly, turned over, and resumed his regular breathing. I turned with him. Laid my face against his back and curled my body around his cool buttocks. What could his mother have been feeling to make her throw herself out of a bed? I'd known her for such a short time: just long enough to idolize her. What could justify such risk? Money? What good would money be if she died in a fall, or crippled herself for life?

Greg didn't stir again until the whistle for the early shift woke us. We lay on our sides facing each other and I kissed his forehead.

"When she got home from Bellingham," he said in a low voice, "she seemed fine. Arturo said she was quiet, but all right."

"She was quiet in Bellingham, too," I said. "Withdrawn." I pulled the tail of my nightgown out from under his leg and tried to visualize a nervous breakdown. "How does she act?" I asked. "I mean, how does she display—"

"Lots of crying. It's happened before. She gets in a rage, rocks back and forth. Then cries. Then talks a blue streak. Doesn't want to take her medicine." He got out of bed.

"Do you want some coffee?"

"I'd better go over and see how she is. Give Arturo a hand."

"It won't take long to make coffee," I said. "You can telephone." By now I was up and dressing, too.

"Okay."

"How can you tell if a person has had a breakdown or is just—exhausted?" I asked. "She goes at such a pace. Maybe she just needs to think about things."

"This is not the first time, Virginia."

"It's the lawsuit that precipitated her . . ." I refused to say *breakdown*. Period of reflection, maybe. A major letdown. Grief and rage after a massive disappointment. I decided not to say anything. What did I know? She was his mother, not mine.

"Damn hospital," Greg said, and shot one leg, then the other, into his Levis. "The bastards led her on, then pulled the plug."

"Morgan Desmond?"

"That's the one. He's all talk."

"That was my opinion."

"How do you know him?"

"I played for their Christmas party." I pulled a sweater from the bottom drawer of the dresser. "What does the hospital have to do with it?"

"Desmond and his lawyer told Mom they would bring in other plaintiffs against the convalescent home."

"But if she lied . . ."

"I have to speculate on some of this," Greg snapped. He walked through the studio and into the living room. I followed in my stocking feet. "Arturo has to speculate, too," he added at the kitchen door. "No one tells us anything specific, least of all Mom."

"She's failed," I murmured. "She hates to fail."

"Who doesn't?" Greg snapped again.

"That must be why she plays up to the Desmonds."

Greg went to the sink and began making coffee. I got cream from the refrigerator and sat down at the table. Outside the window, the rainspout dripped into its mud hole two stories below. "That, and she thinks the Desmonds have class."

"And she doesn't?"

"She still feels like a poor girl in Cincinnati," he said irritably. Beneath the impatience I detected embarrassment. The embarrassment of pitying one's mother. "She feels she deserves more—of everything." He set two cups on the table. "She never feels appreciated enough."

"Arturo seems to appreciate her."

"He comes closest."

"I appreciate her, but she never seems to notice." I cleared away a tremor in my voice and we looked at each other in mutual pain. Greg began pacing from the table to the sink and back again. His curly hair stuck out all over his head, and his lean frame, usually sinewy and taut, now looked merely thin.

"Mom's a social climber," he said. "She tries to mingle with the elite. And the elite let her down." We left unspoken the obvious fact: the elite had been lied to. "She doesn't foresee the implications of what she does," Greg went on. "She decides she needs money and comes up with these bizarre ideas."

I thought of the Central America trip. "Buying and selling drugs?"

"A half-assed plan," he said. "Some scheme from the watery underside of Hilliard. Some idiot with a boat who watches too many movies. You're living in a picturesque old hotel, Virginia, taking piano lessons and playing Bach and Beethoven. But if you look, you'll see something more; something hidden." He checked the coffee. "She'll end up being hurt. She'll never get me to go along with it."

"It doesn't worry her, breaking the law?"

"When Mom's in one of her frenzies she makes her own laws." He went to the hook and took down his coat.

"Aren't you going to have your coffee?"

"I'm sorry," he said. "I'm keyed up. I'm going to the boat, then see my mother, then teach class."

"I'll walk with you," I said. "The coffee can wait."

I got my coat and gloves and the key to the old hotel. Damp, gray air seeped up the stairwell from the gap under the front door. At street level I closed and locked the building behind me.

39

"Careful," Greg said when we reached the docks. "These wet planks are slicker than snot."

When I looked up from our slow progress toward THUNDER, I saw a figure at the far end of the dock, a tall figure swirled in the gray mist of distance, an aloof figure I knew well. I had an irrational longing to run toward it, take the hand with its complex of tendons and muscles and walk to a pleasant place where crying and smiling and sharing come easily. I longed to remake her past so that everything worked out well, bringing an ending as grand and fine as she.

Greg set off quickly. He slipped on a wet plank, caught himself, and moved more slowly toward Twilah who stood facing out toward the channel. I had the awful feeling she was going to jump: that she was considering it in a disinterested way, rather unconscious, in the way a musician works toward the last measure of a piece before actually reaching it. Greg took a long time getting to her. Even when she must have heard him behind her, she didn't turn. He reached for her arm and they began the slow return together.

When they reached THUNDER, Twilah gave me a blank glance. She doesn't recognize me, I thought.

"Hello, Virginia."

"Hello, Twilah." I couldn't think what to say. She didn't like the boat; she didn't like this end of town. Seeing her here was odd.

"Does Arturo know where you are?" Greg asked.

"I left him a note. He was asleep." She sounded like herself, but her face lacked animation. "I'm better now. I hope I didn't worry you."

Greg smiled a relieved smile. "Oh, Mom, we did worry about you." He gave her a long, hard hug. "Do you want to board THUNDER?"

"For a minute," she said. "I just came down for a walk and to see you."

"Actually, I wasn't planning to stay," I said. "There are some things I need to do this morning."

"Come in," she said, and Greg nodded agreement. The three of us stepped into the cockpit and Twilah and I waited while he unlocked the cabin door. Inside, she seemed to forget I was there. Greg made coffee for the second time that morning, glad, I thought, to be running water and clunking around with the coffee can.

"I haven't touched the piano since the audition," I said by way of conversation. I really didn't know how to talk with her about anything except music. She didn't respond. I wondered again if there had been some kind of break or just unbearable disappointment. Perhaps this is what a 'breakdown' looks like, I thought. Unremarkable. Merely an absence of person, not a presence of craziness.

I longed to see her angry, bossy, supercilious, anything to show she felt emotion. This colorless walking to the end of a pier, staring at the water, turning back without either cooperation or resistance, this was emptiness. Absence.

The coffee on the hot plate boiled. Percolating, it smelled sharp and fragrant, but when we drank it in the silent cabin it went down hard. Stale cookies, English biscuits in an imported tin, didn't sit well, either. Greg tried to chat with his mother, but it was tough going. Finally he just started talking about his class, mostly in response to questions from me. I thought: *If only Greg would talk to her about— oh, Arturo, the apartment, any little personal thing, she might respond in some way.* But at moments when he might have caught her attention, he veered off to discuss the heating point of steel or the BTU's of his forge. He lost himself in the subject, in the details of blacksmithing. He referred to his 'craft' rather often, which, in view of her artistic ambitions for him, was not as sensitive as it might have been. Perhaps he instinctively felt that friction, even combat, might be the way to rouse her. Or perhaps he simply didn't know how to talk to his mother.

Twilah interrupted him in the middle of a sentence about melting points, and touched my bracelet, the Damascus steel bracelet Greg had made and given to me.

"This is quite beautiful," she said. She turned it around once on my wrist. I offered to take it off so she could see it closely, but she gestured for me to leave it on. "It's a work of art. Did Greg make it?"

I nodded.

"You are an artist, Greg," she said. "Not a welder." It was not the time for him to disagree with her. The point was, she was talking. Saying anything at all, and with some of the old fervor. But Greg was not his mother's son for nothing.

"It's beautiful because it performs a function well," he said. "It decorates. It is no more beautiful than a well-made tool." He was insistent. Again, I thought, perhaps he knew what he was saying. Perhaps he was merely trying to bring her to life. A good argument for the circulation, so to speak.

I finished my coffee. "Why don't I let you two talk for a while," I said. "I need to get back. Arturo might wonder where you are, Twilah. I can call, if you like, and let him know."

"He knows where I am," she said. "But suit yourself." The sentence hummed with some of the old brusqueness and I wanted more: give us back our sharp-tongued Twilah. Climbing the dock, holding onto the rail so I wouldn't slip, it occurred to me that Greg knew exactly what he was doing. Get her dander up, stimulate her interest; her innate combativeness.

*

I'd been back in the old hotel for maybe thirty minutes when the street door opened and Greg sang out, "Virginia!" I went to the landing. He and his mother were climbing the staircase to my rooms. "I see you decided to disembark," I said.

Twilah reached the top step. She smiled. "I thought you might need a piano lesson."

"I have a welding class waiting for me," Greg said from halfway up the stairs. "Can you drive Mom home?"

"Of course."

Twilah straightened her shoulders. "I don't need a ride," she said. "I'll walk." She climbed the rest of the way upstairs, hung her parka on the hook, and seated herself at the table.

"I'm drinking everybody else's coffee and tea this morning," she said. I took the hint and put on the kettle.

"Are you hungry, Twilah? Can I fix us some bacon and eggs? Or hot cereal? I have hot cereal."

"I used to love hot cereal," she said. "I haven't had any in years."

I filled a saucepan with water. Twilah grew quiet again. In a few minutes the cereal boiled, and I stirred it until it was thick. Feeling motherly, I set her bowl in front of her with spoon, brown sugar, and milk. I was out of raisins. The cereal, lying in the bowl like a steaming, tweedy rug, reminded me of school days with Lawrence and Matt: orange juice, last-minute drill for a spelling test, the morning news.

"This reminds me of cooking breakfast for the kids when they were little," I said.

"Now their father cooks their breakfast," Twilah said. "You should be home cooking for them instead of here cooking for me." The sentence hung in the air, logical, well-constructed, a perfect parallelism. Perfect criticism. "If your kids don't turn out, you'll have no one to blame but yourself."

"Oh, they'll turn out," I said. "All children turn out. Maybe not the way their parents want them to, but they turn out."

"They need their mother."

"They have their mother," I said, furious with guilt and defensiveness. "I was with them every day for their first eight years. Nine years. And I'm with them a lot now, too; just not every day in every way. I'm not underfoot every day, Twilah!" I shot back all the confusion and blame I felt from several directions, most notably my own heart. "Anyway, they're wonderful guys," I finished up. "Perfectly wonderful."

"Being away from them, it would be easy to idealize them."

Not only am I wrong for moving away from my children. Now I'm wrong for idealizing them. Loving them too much. The conclusion is that Ron knows them as they really are and loves them just the right amount. I am thus out-mothered by him. Out-womaned. Out-manned, too. Because what have I to show? A choppy little freelance career filled with job hops and mounting mileage broken up by several months in an old hotel in a broken-down town taking piano lessons from a has-been musician, all the while idealizing my children from a distance and losing touch with reality in the process. I wanted to scream and kick, thereby proving myself not only unwomanly, unmanly, but psychopathic as well. Pushed to extremes by a woman who wasn't doing such a hot job of managing her own life.

"I've upset you," Twilah said. She took a bite of cereal, so calm, so regal, delivering opinion on my motherhood: she who couldn't come down to her son's boat without first having a nervous breakdown. She who couldn't affirm his creativity, his excellence. Who hovered over his dreams like a tall, cold presence.

"Yes, you've upset me." I reached out for Twilah, my teacher, the woman I'd tried to turn into a mother. "I've lost a great deal," I confessed. "My boys have lost a great deal, too."

"Of course they have."

"But," I said, whispering, my throat dry, a spring of water behind my eyes ready to run, "if I'd stayed, growing more and more unhappy, we would have lost a great deal, too."

"So you come up to Hilliard and upset *us*."

She stood, marched over to the coat hook, pulled something out of her coat pocket, and walked back to the middle of the kitchen. She beamed at me, powerful with revenge. "I found these on the boat," she said. Right there she dropped a pair of my underpants on the linoleum floor. I faced her, as frozen as the glutinous cereal in the bottom of Twilah's dish. She gestured toward my bracelet but her eyes were on the underpants. "You can wear 'em on your other arm!" The point of the entire scene gathered like the head of a boil: "I'm the best piano teacher you'll ever have!" she shouted. "And all the time you were seeing my son behind my back!"

I looked at my underwear lying on the floor, crumpled and unsightly, needing a wash. I'd slept with her son and forgotten my pants. She could not endure it.

"What Greg does is his own business," I snapped. "He can return my underwear if it bothers him. I don't remember leaving them. They may not even be mine!" But that wasn't the point. She wanted them to be mine.

She looked at me with contempt, then put on her coat and started down the stairs. "In spite of his upbringing," she said with lady-like articulation, "he always has aimed low." She stepped on one of Marguerite Cleary's starfish. I heard it crunch.

"Broken starfish, broken bones!" I shouted over the banister like a child. She stopped and looked up. "You're going to run out of bones, Twilah!" I yelled down at her. "One hip for Marguerite, one hip for me!"

But after she slammed the door to the street, it was her words, not mine, that echoed in the stairwell and reverberated through my rooms: *Aimed low, aimed low, aimed low* . . . I knew how to fill in the rest. She'd made sacrifices, scraped together cash, left for months at a time buying whatever she bought from Central America. She'd played concerts as if they were one-night stands, she'd given piano lessons to snotty children with no talent so Greg could go to school dressed like the other kids. She had exposed him to the best in music and literature only to have him choose metalwork, welding, a sailboat for a home, first an attendant in a convalescent home for a girl friend, then a divorced woman who didn't have custody of her children. Alone in a life of effort and disappointment, surviving one inundation after another, watching each new, higher wave approach from the open sea, she grasped at objects floating by. Everyone, even her son, turned out to be flotsam and jetsam.

Something else, too. I understood what Twilah was missing with her son: breathing room. She'd had no time to breathe between waves, and neither had Greg. My longing for Matt and Lawrence was eased by the knowledge that they were breathing on their own. I was already letting them be themselves. It was the only way for me to love them now.

40

IN THE EVENING I went down to the docks. The clinking of halyards made lonely music, like chimes still playing after the rest of the orchestra has left. The winter sunset disturbed the world with its bright pink-orange, a forge where all material was changed, liquefied, and hammered into new shapes: old stars made fresh nightly, and a moon that doesn't stay the same, and burning debris that startles anyone who sees it.

I was surprised to see Greg. I'd expected him to be with Twilah and Arturo, but he was crouched in the dinghy, bailing. Always bailing up here where the winter rain seldom stops falling; where the dark seems always to be wet.

"Your mother is furious with me," I said softly.

He continued the rhythmic emptying. "She's furious with everyone."

"She found some underwear of mine on your boat. That is, I guess it's mine. I'm sorry."

"She went looking for whatever she could find," he said. "It's all too much for her, you and me together, the Desmonds fat and happy, you making it into the piano competition."

"I placed?"

"They notified her today."

"It's a compliment to Twilah," I said, feeling no special joy at the news.

"She's forgotten that."

"She's exhausted," I said, still mouthing the platitude, though

I didn't believe it anymore. Now I knew she was malicious and possessive as well as tired.

Greg slowly stood and the dinghy rocked, then stabilized. He stepped onto the dock. The curls at his hairline were damp with mist. "I don't think I realized how hard my mom has always tried," he said.

"Tried . . ."

"Just tried," he said irritably. "Tried to make a good life for the two of us. To be a good mother. To make Arturo happy. To get money, to keep music and art alive, to hang onto me."

"How are you holding up?"

"I feel ragged," he said. "I hope she comes to grips with this thing pretty soon. Arturo and I can't do it for her."

"You can listen to her," I said. "You mean more to her than anyone. Does she have a doctor?"

"She's a tough old bird. She doesn't want to see a doctor. She'll come to herself."

"A person can only hold so much anger."

"She used poor judgment when she . . . rolled out of that bed. I'll never understand where these ideas come from."

"Does she need money that badly? Badly enough to risk harming herself?"

"Arturo's got a trust fund from his family," Greg replied. "It's enough for a modest way of life."

"Your mom doesn't want a modest life," I said. "That's her strength."

"And her weakness." There didn't seem to be much more to say. We'd covered it. We turned to board THUNDER. The sunset was gone, the fires had died, leaving a faint orange line: the horizon was a lid closing on Hilliard and the Sound.

41

My departure for Seattle was anticlimactic. Greg was away at a blacksmith's conference. Since his mother's breakdown, the temperature of our relationship had cooled. Twilah was unaware I was leaving; at least, I hadn't told her. I packed clothes, linens, and music into my two-door Plymouth and drove out of Hilliard. I didn't take a last look at the ship being built in the channel across from the hotel, or memorize the specimens lining the stairs. I didn't entertain any *this-has-been-a-remarkable-period-in-my-life* thoughts as I passed the 'Come Back and See Us' sign on the way out of Hilliard.

The renters of my cottage had left the four rooms and small sun porch relatively clean. Moving back in was swift and I felt almost that I'd never been away. But the boys and I were offstride. They resented me all over again, as if the divorce had just occurred.

"We can't stay with you this weekend. We have a game on Saturday," they would say.

"No problem," I would answer. "We'll go to the game."

"But we always go out for pizza with the team."

"You can go out for pizza with the team."

"Then we always go home and have another game in the back yard."

"Well, you can't do that on the Saturdays you're with me, that's all."

"Jeez, Mom." Looks of anguish and self-pity.

Or,

"We always have Cokes with our hamburgers."

"Dad lets us watch TV before we do our homework."

"It's more fun at Dad's," et cetera, et cetera. I was understanding. After all, I'd gone away, I hadn't been there when these patterns were developed; I had no place in them.

Finally, on the third week of complaints, I'd heard enough. "Nothing's perfect, boys," I said. "Are you saying you don't like it here? You don't want to visit?" They wouldn't go that far. "Because if that's what you're saying, forget it. I want you here, Dad wants you here, it's all been agreed to, and you're too young to change the arrangements. Talk to me about it a few years from now." I surprised myself with the authoritative speech. Surprised them, too. Silenced them, as a matter of fact. A stronger mom: one who made strong speeches, anyway.

And when I told Ron I thought Matt was too young to go hang-gliding with a friend and his father, both of them were angry.

"It was easier when you were in Hilliard," Ron said irritably. But he told Matt no. I felt he was privately relieved. But not Matt.

"It was a chance in a lifetime," he stormed at me the next time they came to spend the night.

"Believe me, Matt," I said, "you have a long lifetime ahead of you and there will be more opportunities to hang-glide." Lawrence listened thoughtfully. I asked Ron if they did the same thing with him; if perhaps they were playing both ends against the middle.

"No," he said coolly.

Contrary to what Ross had told me, he began to give me jobs. If Ms. Liknel, the owner of the only agency in Hilliard, called with a job, I usually took it. I liked working in the north counties where ferries nose between islands with a dignity they aren't aware of; where, in spring, commercial tulip fields explode through the earth's crust in row upon row of lush color; where Canadian geese populate pastures along the road like immense creatures that are too large to be birds. When I finished a deposition or a pro tem court assignment, I often stopped to see Greg or to have a piano lesson with Twilah. As time passed, the cruel words she and I had shouted at each other passed, too. She'd been ill; I'd been dependent. For both of us, music took precedence. And there was this: if I placed well in the Bellingham competition, it would be a coup for both of us.

I invited Greg to come down the first weekend in April to meet my kids. He called the Wednesday before.

"Mom wants to ride down with me," he said. "She thinks you should have another piano lesson."

I hesitated. "She won't like seeing us together, will she?"

Greg hesitated, too. "I'd rather she didn't come. But . . ." He trailed off.

"Come on ahead," I said. "It will be good to see both of you. You can stay over another time." My voice dropped. "I'm disappointed. I miss you, Greg. I wanted to spend the night with you."

"I'm lonely, too," Greg said simply. "Come back."

The delicious, troubling realization swept over me: choices may have to be made. I stood at the telephone, warm for him, responding to him.

"Can you drive back to Seattle the next day?" I asked. "By yourself?"

He thought a moment. "Yes," he said. "I'll see you Sunday. Alone." I hung up and remained where I was beside the kitchen table, staring out the window at the stand of firs in my back yard. I was surprised my erotic feelings for Greg weren't setting the pine needles on fire.

42

TWILAH LOOKED SPLENDID. Matthew and Lawrence stared at the long, patchwork skirt, the clogs, the heavy squash blossom necklace and turquoise rings.

"Virginia, how are you?" she exclaimed. "Hilliard is so unmusical without you." Her strong, melodious voice mesmerized the boys. She held her head high, parting the air inside my little house with her bony face and the high ridge of her nose. Greg followed behind.

"We need to clear the living room for the piano lesson," she announced after ten minutes of conversation. The boys exchanged a quick signal that meant *let's watch TV in Mom's room*. Greg had seated himself in the corner chair while his mother talked. I saw him glance at the baseball gloves and bat lying by the front door.

"How about some batting practice?" he asked the kids.

"There are too many trees in Mom's yard," Matt said.

"Her street's not a cul-de-sac," said Lawrence. "It's not safe."

Greg looked at them in mock puzzlement. "There's a school two blocks from here," he said. "I drove past a whole ballfield."

"It's not our school," said Lawrence.

"Sure it is," said Greg. "It's the taxpayers' school. Your mom's a taxpayer." I'd been trying to get the boys to use the neighborhood playground even before I went to Hilliard. "But Mom," they'd say, "it's not our school." Or, "The basketball hoops are too high, too low," et cetera.

Greg got out of his chair, picked up the bat, and went out on the porch. The boys looked dubious but picked up their gloves and followed, pounding the pouches of their mitts.

When the screen door slammed behind them, Twilah seated herself at the piano and began to play a Chopin prelude. It was the first time I'd heard her play a piece through.

"Beautiful," I breathed when she'd finished.

"I thought you ought to know I do actually play," she said. "I've been practicing all week at the church." She still didn't own a piano and I wondered why she hadn't bought one for herself. Perhaps she didn't want to spend Arturo's money for something only she would use; maybe she was too proud to own a piano that was less than the best. She settled herself on the straight chair I'd placed beside the bench and motioned for me to begin. I warmed up with chromatic scales.

She stopped me halfway through a Bach fugue for a note-by-note analysis of four bars. "You're just making sounds here instead of music," she said. "You must understand the structure."

She was pleased with the Beethoven. "It's nearly ready," she said, making it sound like something in the oven. "Get the whole thing memorized and we'll see where we stand."

"It *is* memorized," I argued.

"No, it isn't. When it's firm, your interpretation will fall into place. You're still unsure. The playing is spotty."

"Spotty?" I thought I'd mastered the sonata, that I couldn't play it any better.

"It's at a high level," she explained. "A high level of spottiness." She shot a glance at my dejected face. "That's a compliment," she added.

We went on with the lesson, I, as usual, stunned by the standard to which she held me. She kept raising the wire.

Near the end of the lesson she put her hands in her lap and turned to me. "Do you want me to come to the competition with you?"

"Of course," I said immediately. "I need you." I put my hand over hers. Her face softened and frown marks smoothed out over the bony plate of her forehead. I can't say she smiled. Since what had been called her breakdown, she didn't smile often.

"Any success I have is because of you," I said. "You should be there." But I'd left my hand on hers a moment too long; my emotion went too deep. She shrugged sharply and looked away.

While we cooked dinner together, spaghetti and meatballs, she told me about piano competitions, students and teachers gathering and disbanding in the lobby of the concert hall, the audience changing each time a new contestant played. She talked while I crumbled oregano into the tomato sauce, tore up bay leaves, cranked the peppermill.

"Isn't that about enough pepper?" she asked.

I stopped grinding and we laughed. As long as we talked about music we were happy. We touched shoulders. Bumped into each other with no *excuse-me's*. She didn't shut down when I asked about music, she didn't get angry or give me to understand I was overstepping a line when the subject was music. She didn't tell me it was none of my business.

Twilah went to the front room. "The boys must be having a fine ballgame," she called back, as if our sons were all the same age. I joined her at the screen door where we stood looking out at the street. Afternoons had begun to lengthen, and at six o'clock it was still light. The forsythia bush by the porch was ready to bloom; limbs and branches of trees all over the city—alder, maple, Lombardy poplar—were knobby with buds; firs extended their bright green candles, fresh and upthrusting, at the ends of gray needles. We sat on the porch step and waited for our ball players. Finally, when it was too dark to see, Greg and the boys came swinging down the street, their voices floating ahead of them. Sweaty and grass-stained, they took turns washing up, then sat down at the table with damp hair.

"How was the field?" I asked when we'd all helped ourselves

to food.

"Great," said Greg. "These guys really know how to handle a ball." He dug into his spaghetti. So did the boys. Mixed with the steam and smell of the tomato sauce was some scent, some atmosphere coming off my kids and Greg: a cooling-down after hard play, the camaraderie of men and boys. I looked at Twilah to share my pleasure.

But, "Don't slurp," she said once to Matt who was sucking up a spaghetti strand. The criticism stung him. Matt tried to do things right. I'd watched him roll the length of spaghetti around his fork. At the last minute he'd lost it.

"A minor slippage," I said, and smiled. He didn't smile back.

"Sit up straight," she said to Lawrence. I expected her to tell Greg to clean up his plate. The kids withdrew from her. Greg ate in neutral silence. Not only had I not gotten to be alone with Greg, but the dinner was going to hell.

"Do you have a game this week?" I asked the boys.

"Just practice."

"Who's your coach?"

"Brian's dad."

"What position—"

"Catcher, Mom."

"Have some salad. There's more bread in the oven. I should have lit the candles tonight, the ones you guys gave me for Christmas," I babbled. *Candles, wine, the beginning of the baseball season, the piano competition* . . . No one helped with conversation. What a grim group, I thought. But I blamed Twilah. Without her heavy comments, dinner would have felt like family. We needed Arturo: he knew how to nudge his wife out of a bad mood.

"Where's Arturo this evening?"

"Working at home," said Twilah.

"He said to say hi," put in Greg.

"Hi, Arturo," I said. After another silence I launched into a recipe I'd seen for spaghetti with snow peas and Chinese greens and duck.

"Good grief," said Twilah. I didn't mention that if I ever prepared it, or anything else, for that matter, I wouldn't invite her. Come to think of it, she hadn't been invited to this dinner.

After they left for home, the boys went into my room to watch TV. I'd just begun washing dishes when I heard the screen door close softly. Greg returned to the kitchen.

"Did you forget something?" I asked.

"This," said Greg, and put his arms around me. He kissed my neck. I lifted my soapy hands out of the sink, and, still reaching around me from behind, he rinsed them for me under the tap, then slipped his hands under my blouse. I twisted hard toward him and we kissed in a series of hot, rushed pecks. The children, Twilah, any of them could walk in. We had to stop.

"Tomorrow," he whispered.

"Tomorrow." I heard the screen door close again and leaned against the counter, happy and weak with desire.

But he called Sunday morning. "I'm afraid today is off," he said.

"What's happened?"

"Who is it?" Matt asked from the breakfast table.

"It's Greg."

"Tell him to bring a glove," said Lawrence. "And a hardball."

"Something's come up," Greg said. He sounded far away, farther than Hilliard.

"Are you in Hilliard?"

"I'm in Hilliard," he said. "But I'm leaving right away for Bellingham."

"Greg! I've been driving up to see you."

"I know," he said. "Of course, you had to drive up anyway."

"Don't you want to see me?"

"I want to see you."

We waited through a strained silence.

"One of my students is setting up a forge at the Bellingham crafts fair," he said. "I just found out about it."

A student.

"Do they expect you to jump?" I said. "Not have any previous commitments?"

"This is really important," he said. "It's his first demonstration."

"Well . . ."

"I can't drive fifty miles in opposite directions at the same time. I have obligations to my students." He softened. "You'll be up again."

"Right," I said.

"Virginia?"

I waited.

"You live in Seattle. I live in Hilliard. This is going to happen a lot."

"Sounds like a promise."

The boys looked at me. "He can't come," I said after we'd hung up. I sat down to breakfast, picked up my fork and laid it down again. It didn't seem possible Greg was doing this to me. Hadn't he known about the demonstration in Bellingham when he'd kissed me last night?

"I think I like Greg more than he likes me," I said to the kids. They made embarrassed eye contact with each other, then looked back at me.

"I really thought he'd drive down today," I said. "He told me he would. And he was going to play baseball with you again."

"He'll come some other time, won't he?" asked Lawrence.

"I hope so, Lawrence," I said. "I really hope so." But I was afraid he wouldn't. He'd visited once; brought his mother; played with my sons; eaten my spaghetti; come back for a quick kiss while *You Know Who* waited impatiently to be driven home. Maybe that was all I could expect. Going out of his way was something Greg might not do. His mother was always there in the background or foreground, ready to have a crisis or crack a bone.

She'd ruined him for me or any other woman.

43

The morning of April 21st broke clear and sunny. On this of all days I could have used a quiet, poetic fog, a softly dripping rain—but no, it had to be bright and sunny. I dressed carefully for the competition: long skirt to fall over the piano bench, I hoped, in a graceful drape: white silk blouse with full sleeves narrowing to a wristband. Soft effect, no constriction. The kids were up before seven, not too happy about spending Saturday in Hilliard and Bellingham, yet considerate enough to dress and eat promptly when I reminded them of my 10:30 spot in the piano line-up.

"Look on it as a crucial game," I said. "It's the piano league, and I'm in the play-offs." They took the unusual step of making their beds and brushing their teeth without being reminded, which proved to me what I'd suspected all along: they had an internal set of high standards willingly applied when they thought necessary.

On the drive north, the weather suited me better. Clouds built on themselves, silver-gray and luminous, their centers dark with threat, change, resolution. Dominant to tonic. Major and minor. Rain chords.

"What time do you play?" Lawrence asked from the back seat.

"Ten-twenty-five, to be exact," I said.

"How's come not ten-thirty?" Matt asked.

"Ten-twenty-five is harder to remember," I said. "It's a test."

His mind on numbers, Matt learned forward and looked over my shoulder at the speedometer.

"Do you know what 'MPH' stands for?" he asked.

"Yeah," I said. "Do you?"

"Yeah." He turned to Lawrence. "Hey, Lawr. Do you know what 'MPH' stands for?"

Lawrence thought for a moment. "Me punch here," he said, and slugged Matt in the shoulder.

"Cut it out!" I yelled over the wrestling. "Back in your seatbelts! Do you want us to have an accident?"

By eight-thirty we were in Hilliard, knocking on the door to the Chans' apartment. I introduced the boys to Arturo while Twilah finished dressing.

"So you're accompanying your mother to the competition," said Arturo, studying Matthew and Lawrence with interest.

"She plays at ten-twenty-five," said Lawrence.

"Ten-twenty-five," said Arturo. "How curious. Why not ten-thirty?" The boys shrugged and smiled.

"We have plenty of time for a second breakfast or a cup of coffee," I said. "Would you like to join us, Arturo? Send us off?"

"I have much to do today," he said. The boys followed his glance to the desk at the window. "But I do 'send you off,' as you say, with my very best wishes."

"Thank you, Arturo." We stood quietly, wrapped in the man's courtesy. The door to the bedroom flew open and Twilah strode into the room, wearing loose velvet trousers with a red cummerbund and an embroidered blouse. I took in a breath, dazzled all over again. She reached for my hand; kissed Arturo good-bye; patted the boys on the head.

"Ready for a day of music?" It was half question, half exclamation. The boys looked doubtful, but they didn't have to answer because she immediately turned to Arturo and said, "I'll be gone most of the day. And who knows? Maybe into the evening. We can never predict"—she gave me an animated glance—"what the new day will bring, can we, Virginia?"

Arturo looked at me and said, with a tolerant but possibly

cautionary lift of an eyebrow, "My wife is rather excited about your competition." He took Twilah's hand in both of his. "The Chinese have a saying: '*Yu Soo Tze Pu Da*'—'Hurrying won't accomplish—hurrying won't get you there,' I believe you would say." Twilah squeezed his hand and gave him a hot little kiss. By the time I turned to go, the kids were already halfway down the stairs. Outside, the weather had changed and we left for Bellingham in a flood of rainwater. The black-and-purple sky opened, Beethoven-like, holding back just enough reserves of lightning, thunder, hailstones, any number of natural disasters, for some future, grander storm.

"Well," I said, cheering up, "this is more like it." Twilah didn't speak until we were out of town. I wondered if this was to be another uncommunicative day. As it turned out, I needn't have worried.

"I recall my first audition, Virginia," she said. "It was in Cincinnati"—she turned to Lawrence and Matt in the back seat—"that's in the state of Ohio, boys. It was during World War II, not long after Pearl Harbor, and my father was on his way to Guadalcanal. Mother was sick and couldn't come to the performance. I was auditioning for a scholarship at the conservatory. Without it, I couldn't enroll. I played Mendelssohn, I remember, and was mortified because I'd worn a street-length skirt and everyone else was dressed to the teeth, suits for the young men, of course, tuxedos for the boys with money, and long gowns for the women. All of them had friends and relatives in the audience, it seemed, but me. I felt disgraced. But the point is"—here Twilah reached for my arm—"I played my heart out, and I earned a full scholarship. I played the pants off most of them." She leaned back in the seat with satisfaction. Behind us, the boys were listening, though they pretended to be more interested in squinting out at the world through sheets of rainwater running down the glass.

"Competition can be painful, even disastrous," Twilah continued. "Some people are not meant to compete. It can be a cruel experience. 'Why must someone be better or worse than someone else?' Arturo often asks me. 'Why not simply enjoy the music at whatever level?' That is because Arturo is a quiet, gentle person who needs no challenge to grow. He grows himself. Some people are like that. I, however, need the stimulation of recognition." Twilah looked at me. "And so do you, Virginia. I know you very well by now. You are an achiever." She looked back at the boys. "Your mother likes to learn new things. She likes to do her very best. And her best is excellent.

"But, as I was saying, competition brings out the worst in some people, the best in others. Someone who lacks confidence"— Twilah turned in her seat again—"as your mother did, boys, when she first arrived in Hilliard, can be destroyed by competition. But once self-confidence grows, it is only natural to want to play for others, show what one can do, seek one's own level. And the level is determined by comparison to others. One craftsman is good or excellent in comparison to another. It's a relative thing. The product—"

"What about joy in work?" I said. I felt ruthlessly competitive. Had felt that way for weeks. It wasn't just divorce and separation from family that had drawn me from Seattle to Hilliard, not simply the desire not to be somewhere, the wish to be somewhere else. It was ambition. Still, I hoped for something more than naked love of achievement. "What about the joy of creating?"

"That's all well and good," Twilah responded. "But to do one's best requires constant striving. Such effort is not always a joy. In fact," she said, "pure joy is a very small percentage of the entire experience. Joy is actually short-lived and occurs at only a few key moments. For example . . ."

I was silenced by the monologue, by its length and intensity. By the truth of what she was saying. Because joy was a small part of the music and mostly it was effort and compulsion, with the occasional rush of profound pleasure. My moments of joy came during a lesson when I played something to Twilah's satisfaction. Perhaps some day—perhaps some day soon—I would be able to set my own standards; to work joyfully, not for someone else's praise, but for my own. Perhaps some day ruthlessness would give way to joy.

I was perspiring.

"Twilah," I said, "I'm trying to stay calm this morning."

"You want me to stop talking?"

"Not exactly," I said. "But perhaps—light conversation. Less intense. Until I've played."

"I see." She moved closer to her door. "The prima donna."

"It's not that. I want to be in control of my emotions today."

"'Me, me, me,'" said Twilah with sudden hostility. "You're always thinking of yourself, Virginia. 'I want this. I want that. I want help. I want to be left alone.'" She unhitched her seatbelt and turned sharply toward me. "Some people can't do what they want, Virginia. Some people have to stay where they are. Some people can't take a leave of absence. Some people can't take piano lessons when they're thirty-four."

I'd thought she understood why I came to Hilliard, even when I, myself, did not. *She*, who had traveled the world looking for imports, had not grasped why I'd come fifty miles north of Seattle.

"You've never been afraid of growth and change, Twilah."

"But it was never at the expense of my son."

"My sons are doing fine," I said, glancing in the rearview mirror. "Their father and I are in agreement about them." The kids listened, embarrassed and interested.

"At least you need to think so."

We were approaching an intersection with a filling station on one corner, a country restaurant on the other. I pulled on the wheel, made a radical swerve into the restaurant parking lot, and unhitched my seatbelt. "You can push me at my piano lessons,"

I said, foot on the brake, index finger in her face, "but that's the only place you'll push me." I opened my car door.

"What are you doing?" said Twilah.

"Making a phone call." With one foot out on the wet pavement, I craned my neck toward the back seat. The boys looked scared. "I'll just be a minute," I said. I raised my eyebrows in a private signal which I hoped they would find reassuring, then took the car keys out of the ignition. Not that Twilah would have driven off. It was just that I didn't know what she would do.

I stood in the rain and dialed Cedar Forge. When there was no answer, I called Arturo. "I'm sorry to interrupt your work, Arturo," I said, "but I wonder if you could find Greg or someone with a car to pick up Twilah."

"What is the difficulty?" he asked in a guarded tone.

"She's talking nonstop. And she's—insulting," I said. "If I thought there was time to drive her back to Hilliard I would, but I have to be in Bellingham by ten." I described the location of the restaurant. If he didn't arrive before I had to leave, I said, I would take her with me and hope for the best. Arturo thought he could be there in half an hour. I hung up the phone, returned to the car, and suggested coffee.

"What in the world for?" said Twilah. "We have a competition to get to. What a ridiculous time to stop for coffee." In spite of her attack a few minutes earlier she said, "There'll be plenty of time for coffee after you win the competition. Because you will win." She clasped my arm. "You have a great gift, and your interpretation is mature. I've told the head of the music department at Western State to make a point of hearing you; that you're a splendid pianist. Older than the average contestant, and therefore more interesting. She'll repeat it. She's a terrible gossip. Can't keep anything to herself. It will be a foregone conclusion . . ." She babbled on. I wiped my forehead and upper lip.

"Let's have some coffee, Twilah." I motioned for the boys to get out of the car.

"I'll wait here," she said. "You'll never get anywhere stopping for coffee every half hour. It's an addiction that gets in the way of discipline, Virginia. What an example for your boys. I think your husband was right in keeping the children. Just go on in. I don't want to join you."

She was still talking when I closed the door. I asked for a table by the window so we could keep an eye on her.

"Why is she talking so much?" asked Lawrence.

"She has moods," I said. My personal opinion was now firm: manic depressive. She needed a psychiatrist. She needed medicine. "She's not always like this," I told them. "I've seen her when she doesn't want to talk at all." The waitress came, and the boys ordered milkshakes and I asked for tea and a muffin. It was four minutes since I'd spoken to Arturo. If he arrived in half an hour, that made twenty-six minutes to wait; forty-five minutes to get to Bellingham; ten minutes to relax before I had to play.

Matt and Lawrence looked out at the car, blew the paper wrappers off their straws, wiggled in their seats. Raindrops hit the restaurant window and ran in separate streams until they merged into a single sluggish sheet that flowed like clear syrup down the plate glass. In spite of the kids jitterbugging around, Twilah sulking in the car (probably still talking, steaming up the windows), I discovered a core of calm inside myself. Once it was clear I wouldn't get through the day without it, that I could easily lose my confidence and momentum because my teacher was unraveling, that core held.

"Stay quiet, boys," I said, "and help your mom. This is one day when I need to concentrate."

"How long are we going to stay here?" Matt asked.

"Until Arturo comes to take Twilah home. She's—unpredictable today," I said. "I can't play in the competition and worry about her at the same time."

"I don't think she likes us," said Lawrence.

"I don't like *her*," said Matt.

"She likes you as well as she likes anybody," I said. "She's just so intense that she doesn't notice how other people feel."

"Why did she come?"

"She's my teacher. Without her, I wouldn't be in the competition."

"I'd rather be home," Matt said.

"Me, too," said Lawrence. My sons weren't enjoying themselves. I wasn't showing them a good time. But it couldn't hurt them to forego enjoyment for a while, could it? Get out of their routine for two days? Part the curtains and glance into a world that wasn't theirs? I touched each boy on the shoulder.

"This is one of those difficult moments we have to get through," I said. "Just lean back and watch. Learn what you can."

The door to the restaurant opened and Twilah, coming down hard on her heels, entered. The eight or ten diners scattered about the open room stared. Her hair was wet, and the velvet trousers and cummerbund had lost some of their pizzazz. She marched to our table.

"How much longer are you going to be?" she demanded.

"One more cup of tea, Twilah. Would you like to join us?" I motioned to the waitress for more hot water. Twilah stood tapping her foot.

"Do you want anything else?" I asked the boys. "How about another milkshake?" Their eyes widened. "Want a Coke? A doughnut?"

"Really, Virginia." Twilah looked at her watch, exasperated. "You can't make this competition go away by sitting in a restaurant all day feeding sugar to your children."

"I feel awful," I lied. "Stage fright." Twilah sat down in the fourth chair and put her arm around me.

"Stage fright is a state of mind which can be controlled," she began. "It is the normal reaction to a misconception about performing. The misguided performer believes people are watching him, criticizing him—"

"Her."

"— and even the audience thinks they have come to hear a particular performer. But what everyone has actually come for is the experience of music. They've come to hear Beethoven. Or they think they have. But what they've really come for is to be taken out of themselves. So you simply concentrate on the experience. You have the experience for your listeners who are not disciplined enough, aware enough, to do it for themselves. This, you see, gives you an edge on them—which they want you to have—an edge you need in order to do your best. It's like actors, teachers, doctors, lawyers, ministers. We all attribute qualities to others that we want them to have; that we need them to have. People want to be fooled. They like to think someone is in charge and can take them painlessly where they want to go."

All this time she'd been leaning toward me, her arm around the back of my chair, talking in a low voice.

"What's interesting," she said, waving away the waitress, "is that when the performer enters a humble state, a disinterested state that is passive yet active, empty yet filled, he can, indeed, lead the audience. That is what the audience wants."

I couldn't tell her that I'd found a calm niche of my own today. It wasn't precisely the one she was describing. It was a center where I would let no one distract me from my purpose, not even Twilah.

An old green sedan rolled slowly into a parking spot facing the window. In the front seat Arturo sat beside a heavy woman in a beret.

"Of course, I don't mean to say the performer doesn't experience nerves," Twilah continued. "He's intense. He's keyed up. No question about it. But he's not frightened. That's the difference between stage intensity and stage fright." She looked out the window with a fulfilled expression and saw her husband coming up the walk.

"What's Arturo doing here?" she asked. Then she turned to me, immediately understanding.

"The prima donna!" She jumped up. Her chair hit the floor. "I'm not needed!" Two tables away the waitress froze with a breakfast plate in each hand, two more riding up her arm. Silence fell over the restaurant.

"You're needed," I said, trying to quiet her. "I need you. But the incessant talk is upsetting me, and I won't be upset today."

Arturo entered the restaurant. He paused in the doorway, folding his dripping umbrella into a baton. He approached our table, calmly picked up the fallen chair, and set it on its feet.

"Janet and I have come to drive you home," he said to Twilah. "Or perhaps we could go for a ride along the bay."

"Janet? Where's Janet?"

"In the car."

I picked up the bill for tea and milkshakes. The boys and I stood to leave.

"Thank you, Arturo," I said. "I'll call on my way home this afternoon."

"Don't bother," Twilah said loudly. Arturo ushered her to the door. Pausing on the step, he opened the umbrella and lifted it above his wife's head. By the time we'd paid our bill and followed them outside, Twilah and Arturo were seating themselves in the back of their friend's old Ford. Arturo left the door open long enough to shake rainwater off the umbrella and fold it into a short baton again. The woman in the beret started her engine. Standing in front of the restaurant, the boys and I caught black smoke pouring out of the Ford's rusted tailpipe. We got into our car. Through the back window I saw Twilah lay her head on Arturo's shoulder. The driver, Janet, cautiously backed out of her parking space, stopped, and ground the gears into first. Then, studying me neutrally through her windshield, she slowly rolled out of the parking lot.

I started my car and entered the road behind her. But instead of following her south, at the first intersection we turned north toward the freeway. In the rear view mirror the green car grew smaller and smaller until it finally disappeared.

"When she knocked over the chair," said Matthew, "I thought somebody'd been shot." This led to nervous laughter on the part of the kids and a rehash of the scene. They were in high spirits, excited by the drama in the restaurant and, I thought, relieved to be away from Twilah.

"What was she talking about?" asked Lawrence.

"How to give a good performance," I said. "That's what it boils down to."

"She's a tyrant," said Matt. His vocabulary surprised me. His concept, so adult, surprised me, too.

"I'm not sure she's actually a tyrant. She has a—strong personality."

"She's bossy."

"What bothers me most," I said, "is that she undermines people."

"What's 'undermines'?"

"Eats away at the foundations. Encourages a person, gives compliments, then follows it up with an attack."

"Oh," said my elder son.

"Still, she's a wonderful piano teacher. That's the thing to remember about her."

"*If* you're taking piano lessons," said my younger son, proving that his brother did not have a corner on adult concepts. I smiled. Beside me, Matt turned on the radio and started listening up and down the dial for rock music until he remembered why we were here, looked at me, and turned it off.

"Is Greg coming?" he asked. I hadn't thought about Greg since we left Hilliard.

"I doubt it. He likes *me* to visit *him*."

"He visited you in Seattle."

"With his mom," I pointed out. "Once."
"Maybe he doesn't like to drive," said Lawrence.
"Does he live with his mom?" Matt asked.
"He lives on a sailboat."
"Let's go see him."

I vacillated, not sure Greg wanted to see us. "We'll stop at the docks on the way home," I finally said. "He'll probably be there. If not . . . there's lots to see. Big fishing boats that go to Alaska. All kinds of boats."

The answer appeared to satisfy them. Rain fell steadily on our car and on the fields along Interstate 5 while music played through my mind, carrying me toward, admittedly, a minor contest where I would be competing with pianists much younger than I. But so what if Bellingham and Hilliard were in an unknown, rural, and remote corner of the continent? I was here. And I'd done it myself. I looked at Lawrence in the rearview mirror, at Matthew beside me. Beethoven may have lit a fire to warm the centuries, I thought to myself, but my little bonfire can produce a glow.

44

We found a parking space at the university and walked across a corner of the campus toward the fine arts building. With fifteen minutes to spare I stopped at the sign-in desk, then went on into the auditorium where I found seats for the kids in the center section. Attendance was sparse, and I would have no trouble spotting the boys from the stage. I sat down between them for a few moments. When I got up to leave, their faces lost expression; they blanked out. I recognized anxiety when I saw it and leaned down to touch each boy.

"Thank you," I said softly. "Clap when I'm done."

"Good luck, Mom." They looked up, it seemed to me, with sad and trusting eyes. Their schoolboy faces melted and, for a moment, I saw them as the babies I had raised. My face may have gone blank, too, with a thought that pierced my breathing: *what's happened to our family?*

Wild grief darkened the room. Because we were still a family. No matter what happened, surely Ron and the boys and I would always be a family. And there was absolutely nothing to be done about it.

Mechanically, I straightened, touched each boy again, and turned and walked back up the aisle, out into the lobby, and down the hallway marked 'Performers Only'.

Outside the entrance I leaned against the wall and cried. Then I blew my nose, pulled the heavy door, and slipped into a dark world that smelled of dust and paint and the magic of theatre. Through a gap in the side curtain, I saw a strip of light, and in that light, polished to a black luster, the piano. Its raised lid and slender legs dominated the auditorium; its elegant keyboard waited coolly, the white and black teeth aligned, as ready to devour as to sing.

Ahead of me, standing with one foot on the rung of a stool, a contestant waited for the timekeeper to give him the high sign. God, he was young. Not much older than Matt and Lawrence, this fellow pianist, musical peer, boy/man in suit and tie.

The audience, such as it was, grew quiet. Suddenly the young man charged onstage, as if the signal had been a pistol shot rather than the timekeeper's discreet nod; as if the gap through the side curtain were a gate onto a track instead of a concert stage. The young man charged into Bach, too. Wonderful fingerwork. Utter bravura. But the phrasing wasn't there. He needed a few years.

I indulged in a moment of self-sabotage: I'll do less than my best, I thought. I'm just a middle-aged woman. This boy/man deserves to win; encourage the children. But ego and the memory of hours and hours of practice took over. We've all worked hard, I thought. They took my registration fee. I'll give them bravura *and* musicianship. Maternal instinct, the encouragement a woman lends children, withered and fell away, and ambition took its place.

The young man now reducing Bach to rubble probably had an entire family rooting for him. Possibly a mother who had sacrificed her ego from the day he was born so he could excel; who took every opportunity to make him look good. Possibly he had sisters who deferred to him. who watched him glorify his school, his family, himself, on playing fields, in classrooms, in recitals. For without a doubt he was a gifted and confident young man, much used to praise.

But suppose this boy had survived and succeeded against odds as great or greater than my own or any girl's or woman's, or any unlucky male's? Still, if he worked hard and had a minimal amount of good luck, his future would be filled with men, boys, women, girls, all expecting him to make something of himself; all watching with interest to see what he could do. True, they would also demand a great deal from him. But here was I, and women like me, willing to take on wide and weighty work, willing to take independent action, run obstacle courses, who were yet made to look atypical, confused, wrong, bad, or psychologically unsound, we ambitious women who would seldom have the support that most men take for granted.

No. I was this boy's competitor. Anything that brought me to a peak, that made me deliver my best and more than my best, I would take on. I wanted to play great music splendidly, and be heard. The boy was just about to land his final blows. Soon it would be my turn. My children would be waiting for me to step out from behind the curtain. That was the kind of support most mothers don't have and wouldn't dare ask for.

The young man stood up from the piano bench. He bowed to scattered applause in the large, nearly empty auditorium, then jogged off-stage with an engaging smile. I wiped my damp hands on my skirt.

"There'll be a five-minute break for people to come into the auditorium," the timekeeper told me.

"My fans," I said. He gave me an interested, curious, then doubtful look. What's this grown woman doing here? What fans? And he was right. Except for my sons who would rather be playing baseball, fans were in noticeably short supply. Greg hadn't come. Hadn't come to see me in Seattle. Hadn't come to hear me in Bellingham. "Just when you begin to count on her," he'd said of his mother, "'bam!' She undermines you." A family trait. *Bam!*

The timekeeper lifted his hand to catch my attention. Creaking seats in the auditorium quietened and grew still and I walked onstage to faint applause, sat down, adjusted the bench, and looked at the keyboard, the beautiful black and white keyboard of the best piano I'd ever played. I plunged into the opening measure. The piano's tone carried me into the stream of the piece. Gradually I forgot about the audience and the contest. I was drugged; drugged with music and ego, and then no ego; I wasn't there. Only music. Hot face, cool hands, perception of time passing, all were at the periphery; on the outskirts of music. I played for what could have been minutes, or could have been seconds. Then I lifted my hands. The piece was finished and I was back.

Silence. I was shocked. They hadn't liked it. Then I heard applause strung out among the poor attendance, a lonely echo against the high walls and ceiling. In my imagination the audience had been large. I smiled out at Matthew and Lawrence, bowed, and walked off-stage. The timekeeper studied his pocket watch. No acknowledgement. No smile. Not even a request for an autograph. *Imagine that.* I walked down the long corridor to the lobby.

"Good, Mom," Matthew said when we met, as planned, in front of the water fountain. They patted my arm, and for the briefest of moments nudged up against me.

"What are we going to do now?" they asked. I laughed. To me, the competition was the culmination of years of work; to them, it was only slightly more important than a milkshake, and insignificant compared to baseball, soccer, basketball, dinosaurs.

"Did you win, Mom?"

"It's too soon to tell. They announce the results at four o'clock."

"Four o'clock!"

"How long till four?" asked Lawence.

"Forever," said Matt.

"Let's look around the campus," I said. "Maybe we can find something interesting."

"I'm hungry," said Lawrence.

"We'll have lunch, then. Early lunch." We stepped out of the fine arts building into weak sunshine. Damp sidewalks crisscrossed this part of the campus and ran like silver ribbons past beds of buttery daffodils. At the student union we found a cafeteria. On a shelf near the entrance I saw one stack of catalogues for the university, another for extension classes. I put one of each in my purse and followed the boys to the grill.

"Are you going to call Greg?" they asked again while we stood waiting for meatloaf and mashed potatoes.

"I don't think so."

"But we want to see his boat."

"We'll stop at the docks on the way back to Seattle. I told you that."

"There's lots of room for batting practice," Matt said, looking out at the wet lawns. "Call him up, Mom. There's still time."

"I don't think he'll come."

"He doesn't like to drive." Lawrence had found an excuse for Greg.

We passed the afternoon restlessly. I suggested we go to the car and get the bats and ball. The two of them could play with or without Greg. We drove down to the fieldhouse. The unstable sunlight had not dried the grass down here, either, and the kids played catch in a corner of the football field, their shoes getting wetter and wetter, while I sat on the first row of bleachers and alternately read, watched them, and tried not to think about the results of the competition.

By four o'clock we were back in the fine arts building for the final ceremony. Strange. I'd played well without Twilah, but now that the results were to be announced, I missed her terribly: I missed her through the welcoming speech, the self-congratulations, the thanks. A frail, white-haired music professor rendered an amorphous Saint-Saens with such gentle feeling that he put the audience into a dream state, a trance broken only when he leaped nimbly from the piano bench to our startled applause.

The chairwoman of the department re-welcomed us, then went on to honor the piano teachers, one by one. Twilah's name was called, but she wasn't there to stand, and no one clapped. The silence isolated my teacher, and thus me. I sat without moving, as humiliated—and yes, angry—as if I'd lost a lawsuit of my own; as if I, too, had to be driven home early. Twilah's behavior, whatever the cause, be it manic-depression, meanness, ego, had brought me to the edge of her anger and shame. And this is just a small part of what Greg must feel, I thought. Pity and shame and anger and grief for his mother who is at the center of his life. No wonder he has nothing left for me.

Scattered bits of thought, glass fragments in a kaleidoscope, held steady for a moment: Twilah will be herself again. We'll resume lessons and everything will be as it was before. Then the colored bits, shrapnel of feeling, came loose, broke apart, flowed over each other again, bumped and ground and splattered, spilled and ran, and came to rest in a new configuration: flawed women. Flawed men. Brave and imperfect people. A quiet generosity toward us all fluttered just out of range of the kaleidoscope screen.

Beside me, Lawrence carefully folded a paper airplane. He dropped it, picked it up, and began creasing the wings again. On the stage the plump, enthusiastic chairwoman, who had to be asked to step back from the microphone and speak at a lower volume, announced the honorable mentions. Ten students ranging in age from grade-schoolers up through seniors in high school passed by in a line to receive their certificates. Next came the third-place winner, a girl of about sixteen who I had not heard play. Lawrence looked at me, put his airplane aside, and cracked his knuckles in anticipation. Matt sat quietly. Perhaps he had been aware all along that I was older, far older, than the other contestants.

Again, I felt equivocal, momentarily ashamed of myself. What would the parents and teachers think if I walked up the aisle to take their child's prize? Strange and selfish woman. Prize-snatcher. Baby-napper.

When the loud and brilliant boy who had preceded me rushed up the stage steps to receive second prize, I knew I had either placed first or been passed over because I was in the wrong age bracket. We all clapped while he shook hands with the chairwoman and received his certificate. We clapped until he had jumped off the stage and run back up the aisle to sit with a large group of people who leaned in toward him and dusted his shoulders with whispered praise. Then they all straightened to see, through narrowed eyes, I imagined, who had placed first.

My heart kicked into action. One large, uneven beat squeezed out blood. Thumped me hard and shifted all the weight in my chest cavity. I am too old to compete, I thought. I'm going to have a heart attack. But my chest straightened out, as it always did in these episodes of arrhythmia, and I was able to hear the chairwoman say, "And now, the Department of Music presents, with pride and with our sincerest congratulations"—here she had to go into a little routine about how difficult it was for the judges to award prizes because of the fact that the general level of technique and musicianship was so high, however, it turns out, they had made a choice, although she seemed loathe to ever say what—and now they were happy to present the highest award, first place—she fumbled for her eyeglasses which hung on a ribbon around her neck and bumped about on the broad shelf of her breast—"first place to—Virginia Johnstone!"

Lawrence turned to me. "Mom!" he said loudly. Matt's knee jerked. I stepped over their feet and reached the aisle. God, it was a long aisle. People stopped clapping before I reached the stage. The chairwoman extended both hands, shook mine with both of hers, then gave me a certificate and an envelope.

"Your playing was exquisite," she said away from the microphone.

"Thank you," I said. "I have a wonderful teacher."

"Twilah Chan?" She began to pump my hand again. "I haven't seen her today."

"I'm afraid she couldn't be here."

"Give her my best. Tell her to visit me."

"I certainly will." I smiled and smiled. The applause tapered off, and by the time I had descended the steps of the stage, she was speaking again. Matt and Lawrence grinned openly when I reached my seat. I grinned back. Someone in the row behind leaned forward and whispered, "Well done."

"—reception for all finalists, their teachers and families, on Sunday, May 13th, at the Department," the chairwoman was saying.

"That's you," I whispered to the boys. "My family. Want to come?"

"No," said Matt. Lawrence shook his head with conviction.

"You've been wonderful," I said. "No more command appearances."

I put my arms around them, but briefly. The thrill of winning was already wearing off for them and they had begun to feel self-conscious. Matt put out his hand for the prizes, so I gave the certificate to one boy, the check to the other. After studying them, trading them, they handed both back to me and acted as if nothing had happened. The chairwoman brought the program to a close and we all stood to leave. On the way out, people stopped to congratulate me, but since I didn't know anyone, I kept moving forward, the kids right behind me.

In the car I put the key in the ignition. Overcome with pleasure, I laid my head on the headrest and asked Lawrence to get the certificate out of my purse. I held it, straight-armed, out to one side and soaked up the honor in a way I hadn't had time to do.

"I knew you were good," Matt said from the back seat, "but I didn't know you were that good."

I pulled the certificate down to lap level. The excitement began to leave me. I couldn't hold the emotional pitch forever, though I would have liked to. My attention span, like the boys', was short. I felt tired. I wanted Twilah to see my certificate; I wanted Greg to be pleased. I was as aware of loss now—Twilah, Greg, Hilliard—as of gain. The boys sensed my mood and grew quiet.

"I miss Twilah," I said. "She deserves most of the honor."

"You're the one who played the piano," Matt said sensibly.

I closed my eyes on tears. "Thank you, Matt."

"If you hadn't gone to Hilliard," Lawrence mused, "this wouldn't have happened." I looked at him to be sure of his meaning. His expression was frank and innocent. I held onto the certificate and check and asked them a question I hadn't, till now, wanted answered.

"Are you sorry I came to Hilliard?"

There was a moment of silence. "It's okay," Lawrence said. "Dad takes care of us." After another moment of thought, "And you learned to play the piano."

"You knew how to play the piano in Seattle," Matt said. I nodded. It was true. Not as well, but I'd played. "I don't like Hilliard," he added.

I sat up slowly. "I need to accomplish something. And I feel a sense of accomplishment in Hilliard and in Bellingham."

"Why can't you accomplish something in Seattle?"

"I probably don't play as well as people in Seattle," I said. "I'd be lost in the shuffle. Anyway, it didn't happen in Seattle. It happened in Hilliard." I looked down at the certificate. "This prize is for lessons at Bellingham, not Seattle."

"You're not staying up here, are you?" Matt asked sharply from the back seat.

"No," I said, looking in the rear view mirror. "But I am going to take these piano lessons. I'm going to claim my prize, Matt."

"It's not that far from Seattle," Lawrence said in a mediating tone of voice. Grateful, I reached over and patted his shoulder. I sat up straight, turned the key in the ignition, and we started the drive to Hilliard. A half hour later the kids were running down the ramp ahead of me while I followed behind, negotiating the perforated metal walkway in high heels. By the time they'd reached the end of the dock, I was just passing THUNDER. The hatch to the fo'c's'le stood open, which meant Greg was either on board or not far away. At the next dock over, fishermen on commercial vessels mended nets, yelled at each other over their engines, listened to radios turned up loud to the same station.

"What are they doing?" Matt asked when I caught up to them.

"I don't know specifically," I said, "but in general they're getting ready to go fishing. They go for weeks or months at a time. Alaska, for instance."

"What do they do with the fish they catch?"

"They unload them onto floating canneries. They process the fish on the water. They don't have to bring them all the way back to port." I was repeating what Greg had told me. I tried to remember other information: mending nets, cleaning and oiling winches, emptying bilges, scraping and painting decks. Blocks. Net reels. The boys turned and started back.

"Stop when you get to THUNDER," I said. They slowed down and began reading boats' names aloud: "MARIANA," "NORTH BY NORTHWEST," "MY LADY," "FRANKENSTEIN AND MIRE."

"FRANKINCENSE AND MYRRH," I corrected Lawrence.

"THUNDER!" they read loudly.

"Greg?" I called. I walked down the starboard side and stopped at the pilot house. The door was open. "Anybody home?"

Greg stepped out on deck. "How's it going?" he said casually. He stood there, half-stranger, half-friend. As aloof as I'd been when I first came to Hilliard.

"How have you been?" I asked.

"Fine. You?"

"I'm fine."

"How are the ballplayers?" he asked. They stood quietly beside me on the walkway between THUNDER and the next boat over.

Now that they could actually talk to him, they'd turned reticent.

"Twilah didn't come to Bellingham today," I said.

He nodded.

"How is she?"

"She took her downers."

"I called you, then I called Arturo."

He didn't respond.

"It would have been difficult to leave her alone while I played," I apologized. "It would have been difficult," I repeated lamely.

He shrugged. "It's not your problem."

"Want to hit some balls?" Lawrence asked. He'd got his voice back. I felt mired—my own 'Frankenstein and Mire'—in self-doubt and uncertainty about what Greg thought of me and whether he wanted us to go or stay.

"We just dropped by," I murmured. "I told the boys about your boat." I turned to them. "We didn't give him any warning we were coming." I sounded ashamed for myself and, what was worse, for my children.

"Sure," Greg said easily. "I could use some ball practice." The air cleared. The world suddenly smelled salty, fishy, and fresh.

Greg looked at my skirt and heels. "How did it go this morning?"

I breathed deeply and held the breath. Every object moved into clear focus. Nothing stirred, and the full pleasure of my award penetrated to the bone.

"I won first place."

Greg put his head to one side and shed the casual acquaintance role. He hugged me like a brother, or maybe like a colleague in work. Trembling, I turned and walked back up the dock, steadying myself in the high heels. The kids were already on the ramp. Greg took my hand for a moment, then released it. He hung back and looked at the rain clouds to the west. "I left the hatch up," he said, and returned to the boat.

"Where's Greg?" said Matt when I reached the car. His face

masked disappointment. He was afraid Greg had changed his mind.

"Closing the hatch. He'll be here," I assured them. When he stepped off the ramp a few minutes later he was carrying a baseball glove.

"I found this in my shop," he said, sliding into the front seat beside me. He slammed his fist into the cracked leather palm. "I used to play a lot of ball," he added. The kids were silent; silent with happiness and admiration.

We drove to Greg's old junior high school and parked as close to the baseball diamond as we could get. All three were out of the car before me. I followed at a leisurely pace to the first row of bleachers where I sat and watched Matt and Lawrence at home plate weighing their two bats, taking practice swings as if getting to know new bats; as if they hadn't had the same bats since last summer. Of course, they didn't have the same bodies so the bats were shorter and lighter now.

Out on the pitcher's mound, which was dark and moist from the day's intermittent rains, Greg practiced his wind-up. No one seemed to notice the damp. The boys' shoes were wet for at least the third time that day. Under a sky that swung from sun to cloud and back again, all three of them slipped and slid, staining their clothes grass-green in the service of sport. I basked in the moment and tried to memorize happiness. Sitting there on the first row of the bleachers, my life in Seattle moved to the background—the outfield, as it were—and music took over. I could pretend to think and plan, but it would be pretense indeed. I had already decided: I was going to study music, and get a degree, if I could.

An hour and a half later, a light shower had turned into major rainfall and we could no longer pretend that night wasn't bearing down on us, stealing this irreplaceable day. We dropped Greg back at the docks.

"Thank you," I said. With all my heart I did not want him to open the car door and step out. I wanted him with us always. At the baseball diamond it had felt like family. Still, sitting there in the bleachers, I'd experienced an exhilarating sense of myself that included mommy/daddy/two kids. To have both family and independence would be bliss. I did not know how to do it. But knew that the absence of either diminished me.

"Good game," said one boy.

"See you later," said the other.

When Greg said good-bye—no touch, no kiss on the cheek, no special sign—I knew what I faced. Greg and I could no longer count each other as the dearest other person, we would no longer drive to Cedar Forge together in his old pickup, we would no longer go down to THUNDER at night to sleep.

He called the next weekend, apparently for no other reason than to ask how I was. I was fine. He was fine. I was working hard. He was working hard. My kids were fine. His mom was fine.

"I need to talk to her about lessons," I ventured. "If she'll teach me."

"I thought you were taking lessons at Bellingham."

"Not until summer term."

"Well, give her a ring when you're in Hilliard."

"Do you ever get to Seattle?" I asked, dropping the conversation one notch below the surface of things.

"Not much. My work's here," he said.

"I almost wish I hadn't come to Hilliard," I said, plunging deeper.

"We wouldn't have met." He paused. "It would be easier now."

"It would be easier now," I echoed and armed myself to make a point. "It's not that far to Seattle," I said. "I've made the drive many times." In the silence I heard a faint voice sawing away on another phone connection. Hilliard had dreadful phone service.

"Usually I say no when people ask me to go out of town," Greg said. "I didn't always, but I do now. I get distracted from my work." His voice dropped. "My work holds me together."

"Well," I said, "when I'm in Hilliard, do I distract you?"

"Yes," he said. "Yes, you do." He adopted a chummy, superficial tone. "I just wanted to tell you how much I think of you and your kids."

"So do you think we should just call it a day?" I said, sounding like the lyrics to some old popular song. He didn't answer; the answer was self-evident. "I'm in Seattle," I said obstinately. "You're in Hilliard. It doesn't seem that far to me."

"It seems a long way to me."

"Is the drive too far?"

"For me, yes. I've made my choices. My work is here. I'm staying put."

"It looks like you want me to do all the changing."

He heated up. "I'm not asking you to change." Pause. "You're changing, anyway," he added. "You were the one who came to Hilliard. I didn't go to Seattle."

His logic was unarguable. He was earth. I was water. He held steady. I was attracted to men who held steady.

"Well, I'll see you sometime in Hilliard," I said. We didn't mention his mom. If Greg fit into my piano study, my music, fine. If I fit into his metalwork, fine. If not, I thought as I hung up the receiver, fine. My heart felt sore, my arms empty, love unattached, sex unused. But on the matter of our relationship, fine. My mind was as clear as his.

45

Ron glanced through the Western Washington University catalogue I'd just handed him; he flipped from back to front, middle to end, beginning to middle. He'd always had a quick grasp of written material, and could finish the editorial page and tell me everything on it before I'd finished the letters to the editor.

"Why do you read them?" he would say. "They're letters from ordinary people who don't know what they're talking about."

"Well, I like ordinary people. It's interesting to know what ordinary people think."

"Not when they're uninformed." Ron would shake his head and devour another page of newsprint.

He handed the catalogue back to me. "Have you told the kids?"

"I thought I'd discuss it with you first."

"What's to discuss?" he asked. "You've already made up your mind."

"I wanted to tell you before I tell them. I'll help them understand my reasons," I said. "I'll help them through this—"

"Your reasons aren't understandable, Virginia," he said abruptly. "Don't bother explaining. Just leave Seattle. Leave the city. Everything will be easier without you. You don't have a place here."

I, who had left him, felt hurt, insulted. I realized he still mattered to me. As long as we had children—which was forever since our children are ourselves and we can barely imagine the universe without ourselves in it; can no more relegate the children, once they've been born, to non-life than we can erase ourselves—Ron and I would never shake loose from each other.

"I'll always be their mother," I said.

"Their mother? You're not here! How can you be the mother of two young boys if you're not here?"

"Perhaps I never was here."

"No, perhaps you weren't."

And why wasn't I? With a nice man, a willing husband and father like Ron, why hadn't I been present? For a moment I doubted my very existence.

He stomped off into the living room. I followed, but stopped where hardwood ended and green shag carpet began. He picked up a heavy glass ashtray from the coffee table and held it in front of him, almost as if he were going to be sick. There was one butt in it. I wondered if Anna had come back.

"Ron—"

"I hate you," he said. "You keep leaving the boys over and over again."

You insisted on keeping the boys! I wanted to shout. *They could be living with me now!* But I only stared at his hatred and believed it. He was shockingly pale and shockingly livid. I loved him and hated him both; I wanted to fall into his arms, and beat him, and kill him. My toes curled at the edge of the carpet and almost catapulted me into my old living room. Suddenly Ron wheeled and threw the ashtray at the fireplace. The music of glass disintegrating filled the room. He looked better immediately. The boys ran down from their rooms where they'd gone as soon as I'd delivered them home.

"What broke?" they asked.

Our family.

They stared into the living room and looked at their father. They hadn't spotted the splinters of glass all over the hearth and rug.

"Your dad and I are having a discussion, possibly a fight," I said. "Now run upstairs and let us be silly adults."

But they stayed until Ron said, "I broke the ashtray. That's all."

I wondered if he and the boys were thinking of Anna. Only when Ron picked up the college catalogue from where he'd thrown it on a chair did the kids go back upstairs, single file and silent.

"How in the world are you going to afford college?" he asked. For a moment his tone of voice, my own fears, convinced me I couldn't. It would be impossible. In my mind I ran over a rough plan for the future, silently reciting it to Ron. I'd forgotten that I didn't owe him an explanation.

"I thought I would sell the cottage," I murmured. The little house, my Seattle house, had been a rental we'd purchased when Ron's parents died and left us money. We'd repainted it, brought it up to code, and become landlords.

"That house is your investment," he said coldly.

"I don't want to sell it," I said, "but I think I have to. It's more useful to me right now than it will be in the future."

"Why do you say that?"

"Because now is the time for change. Now is when I need tuition money."

"You never could see past today," he said. He began to pace between the fireplace and his chair, avoiding the broken glass where it had bounced off the hearth onto the rug. "Past today, hell, past this hour. This minute." He turned on me. "You've upset a family, you've upset two boys, and now you're upsetting your own future."

I walked over to the sliding glass door and looked out on the patio.

"I didn't have to tell you any of this," I said. "I could have called you up and said, 'Oh, by the way, I sold the house.'"

"It really doesn't matter how you do it," he snapped. "The house is gone in any case." I adjusted the strap of my shoulder bag and returned to stand at the edge of the rug.

"How are you going to eat? Pay rent? Car insurance? Gasoline? The kids' support money?"

"That comes out of court reporting income," I said. "But for tuition, I need the house." Before I'd come here it had all been clear in my mind: I would live cheaply, probably in the old hotel—there was no cheaper place anywhere—and work for Liknel Reporters and anyone else who needed a reporter in the counties. Even drive to Seattle for the occasional lucrative job.

"And you're going to study music?" He spat out the word.

"Music."

"Music."

"I can teach," I said without conviction. Maybe play for people, I thought to myself, get work as an accompanist. The truth was, I had as much doubt as Ron. What does a middle-aged graduate do if she's a pianist? Does anyone want to hear her? Does anyone want to hire her?

"This wouldn't have happened if you'd stayed in Seattle," Ron said, following me to the front door. Lawrence had said the same thing, but in quite a different tone. "There's no real competition up there."

"I know that."

"So why don't you take the challenge down here?"

"The lessons this summer are in Bellingham," I said, pivoting and talking loudly into his face. "It's my prize. I won first place in Bellingham, not in Seattle. It happened there."

"You're a child, Virginia. A damn child." He ran his hands through his hair. I so easily saw his point of view. Good man, reliable, fine future at the U., from a good family, and he has to marry a woman who has dissatisfaction built into her.

"Where did the kids go?"

He looked distracted. "Probably watching TV."

"I want to tell them my plans."

"For God's sake, can't you save it for a day or two?" He was stretched very thin. Single dad. His romance with Anna finished, or at least in jeopardy.

"Ron," I said, "would you like me to take the boys?"

"And send them up to Hilliard or Bellingham or God knows where, when you can barely support yourself?" He was yelling now.

"I can handle it. I'm more capable than you realize."

"You can't raise children alone," he said scornfully. "You're not an adult yourself."

"By your definition I hope I'll never be an adult," I shot back. "I hope I'll never lose the courage to change. I don't intend to get stuck!"

"You'll get stuck in the end," he said. "Oh, it may take a while. But you'll get it in the end." Ron was so predictable. Even his deepest feelings came out as clichés. I shouldn't have talked to him. I owed him nothing, yet it was strange how difficult it was to break old dependencies, and I had come with some expectation of encouragement. A pat on the head: *Yes, Virginia, I think it's a fine plan. Yes, sell our rental house. And best of luck in your endeavors.*

I wondered how we'd stayed married as long as we had.

"I'll talk to the kids this weekend," I said. "Are you going to tell them first? Because I'd like to."

"I don't know."

"I'll come see them regularly, just as I did before. There's no need for a major disruption."

"Disruption?" He laughed at me. "You're a walking disruption!"

"Change is disruption," I retorted over my shoulder, and stepped off the porch.

"See a psychiatrist!" he shouted, and slammed the door.

I backed out of the driveway, red in the face. Ron would no doubt be grinding his teeth. I wished I hadn't shown him the college catalogue. I should have told my sons and let my ex-husband find out on his own: told them my decision, uncolored by Ron's jeremiads and predictions of failure, and let them rely on their own common sense and our relationship to adjust to the change. If Ron frightened the boys or made them hate me, I would never forgive him.

But when I told them my decision the following weekend, they seemed neither surprised nor distressed. Lawrence was his usual generous self. Matt, more cautious, took it well. Perhaps Ron had prepared them, or perhaps they'd sensed all along that I would leave again for Hilliard; I wondered how well they knew me.

"I'll drive to Seattle to see you," I assured them. "There will be times, however, when you'll have to come up to Hilliard."

"We can play baseball with Greg," Matt said philosophically. I hoped he was right. As far as they were concerned, baseball season would last forever and Greg would always be on the pitcher's mound. I didn't express any doubt about Greg or the end of summer, about the putting away of bats and balls and gloves. They would find out soon enough. By then something else would capture their attention; that was the way life went with children. I should know. Hadn't Ron called me a child, too?

46

Twilah and Arturo's apartment house looked just as it had the first day I stepped up onto the wide porch, but the weather was warmer now, hot in midsummer. A gaggle of kids rode by on bicycles, damp towels rolled up in wire bike baskets and their hair wet from the swimming pool. I imagined two boys, ten and eleven, chestnut brown hair and clear hazel eyes, riding along with them, no hands, voices piping, "Hey, Mom!"

It had rained the night before. Coughed up by a lawnmower, wet grass lay in clods on either side of the front walk. I stepped onto the porch. No need to read names on the mailboxes this time. I went inside, climbed the stairway to the second floor, and paused on the top step to look over the banister at the same dreary chairs in the entryway below, as dreary as I'd been a half year earlier, and much clearer about their function. Ahead, the dim hallway ran straight to the back of the house. I followed the same dirty runner, colorless in the dingy light that a small window at either end of the corridor still rationed out. Under the same bare light bulb I knocked on Apartment G. Twilah opened the door.

"How are you, Virginia?" Her greeting was restrained, but she herself looked as vivid as ever: snapping eyes, black as—well, as the grand piano in the concert hall at Bellingham. Strong, bony nose, full lips, short and wiry gray hair, and stupendous earrings, silver disks with beads attached like spokes of a wheel, the rays of the sun, and then more disks dangling from those disks, all of which looked grand on her because of her height and the bone structure of her face and her presence. "Come in."

We didn't hug. We both remembered how I'd trapped her at the country restaurant the last time we were together; how I'd sent her home early with Arturo and the woman in the green sedan.

She'd never congratulated me on winning first place.

"So you need another lesson," she said neutrally.

"Always."

I listened for Arturo in the other room. His desk looked tidier than usual, as if he'd finished his book. The green plant had grown in its ceramic pot; it was taller each time I saw it, like my boys.

"So let's have a lesson," she said. I couldn't imagine where. I wouldn't be renting my old rooms for several weeks yet, and Twilah didn't have a piano.

"Where?"

Twilah glanced at me, then away, as if the light I shed was too dim to be of any use. "I have access to many pianos," she said.

"I didn't bring my music," I said. "I thought we'd set up a schedule—"

"Did we set up a schedule the first time you came asking about lessons?"

I shook my head.

"I don't set up schedules," she said. "I just begin."

"My music . . ."

"Really, Virginia. I have music. And if I have no music, I have a memory. So do you." I waited obediently while she walked to a cabinet against the wall, opened the door, and got down on her hands and knees. The hem of her flowing blouse—long enough to be called a tunic—and the edges of her silk scarf brushed the floor in front of the lower shelves as she peered at the volumes packed horizontally, back to cover, cover to back, in columns.

"We'll learn Brahms," she said. "It's time you played Brahms." I reached eagerly for the music she handed up to me, through air that had suddenly grown as buoyant as an ocean. The insults, the hostility vanished, and I was ready again to plunge in, thrash, flounder, float, whatever I had to do to reach Twilah bobbing farther out, farther than I could swim, until I arrived, dripping and breathing hard, squirting salt water in a plume, and shouting, "Teach me Brahms!"

"We'll use the piano at the church," she said. I offered my hand. She took it and stood, brushing the knees of her slacks, the skirt of her tunic, before she closed the cabinet doors. "It's not far."

I remembered the church where I'd originally gone looking for her on a velvety November day that had been almost dark by four o'clock. But now it was summer when you can drive at eight-thirty without headlights, and short sleeves are good all evening. Twilah and I left her apartment house and walked down the street in sunshine. It was a fruity, still afternoon at the edge of the Sound.

I lengthened my steps to keep up with her. We passed houses, two-story frame, with capacious porches across their fronts. A tricycle waited by a door, its front wheel twisted back like a dog scratching itself. In the distance, a semi whined up High Street.

"Perhaps you wonder," Twilah said, "why I don't have a piano." At that particular moment I wasn't wondering anything of the kind. The afternoon held my attention. I was inexpressibly happy to be back in Hilliard.

"Why is that?" I asked as we crossed over to the church.

She began to talk, not urgently, not even fast. Quite without compulsion. In an easy voice she delivered such a well-conceived monologue that I wondered if she'd worked it up.

"It's a question of money," she said. "Arturo is quite serious about going to Guatemala. We're leaving in September. Greg is well-situated here, Arturo's book is completed, and you're taking lessons in Bellingham. There is nothing to hold us. It is the perfect time to leave."

She had mentioned me in the same breath with her husband and son.

"Twilah," I began, "you've meant so much—"

"I actually do not want to go," she continued, rolling over my emotionalism. "We are not wealthy people, Arturo and I. Traveling costs money. Thus, no piano. Thus, a two-room apartment in what used to be a fine home. The building is one step above the old hotel, Virginia; one step only."

"You've made your rooms beautiful."

"Thank you. As I was saying, the Guatemala trip is Arturo's idea. We've scraped together the money. Greg has decided against going with us. He would be a great help, but he has decided against it. It's a buying trip. I buy native crafts and bring them back to sell in the States." She looked at me down the length of her bony nose. "I have contacts in Central America."

Stepping around a cat that had thrown itself into a patch of sunlight, flat as a rug, we approached the side door to the Methodist Church.

"Arturo will be doing research for his next book," she continued, "and I will be financing it."

"Have you ever given piano lessons down there?" I asked as if *down there* were the bottom of the world or even farther.

"No," she said. "Buying is more lucrative." I doubted Twilah bought only stitchery, baskets, and wood carvings. Greg as much as told me she bought dope. For all I knew, she used it. It was a possible explanation for the moody silences, the marathon talk sessions. When she fell apart after the lawsuit, Greg had called it a nervous breakdown. Maybe it had been drugs. I would probably never know. I'd been right about one thing, though: it was none of my business. It never had been. All along, music had been my business.

The short stairway leading down into the church basement was dark and smelled of old hymnals and potluck suppers. Twilah snapped on the lights. We stood in a low-ceilinged hall with a small stage at one end and pictures of Jesus prominently displayed along the walls. Hand-painted signs near the opposite doorway pointed toward the Sunday School rooms, choir loft, nursery. Behind a pass-through window, the kitchen waited for—the Martha Circle, perhaps.

We approached the upright piano backed up against the raised stage at the far end of the room. Twilah pulled out the bench and I brought a folding chair from a stack of chairs in the corner.

"How are the lessons going at the University?" she asked off-handedly.

"I've only had one. The professor isn't as good as you."

"You don't have to flatter me. I know I've grown rusty over the years."

"I'm not flattering you. He knows music, of course, but he doesn't give me a sense that anything is possible." Twilah sat rigidly straight on the metal chair. "With him I never explore new territory, never hear a bomb explode. If you know what I mean."

"I'm not sure I do." She leaned back against the chair. "The way I teach is the way I am."

I tested the pedal, scooted the bench back an inch.

"I'm moving to Hilliard," I said abruptly. "This time it's permanent."

She lifted her eyebrows.

"I've got a job with Liknel Reporters in Vernon."

She reflected for a moment. "Will you be continuing lessons in Bellingham?"

"Yes," I said. "I'm enrolled for the fall as a Junior." Twilah's mouth fell open. I laughed out loud. "Still trying to be a kid," I said.

Her eyes were fierce. "Don't let anybody stop you." When the moment of determination subsided she asked, "Does Greg know you're moving back?"

"I think he does," I answered casually. We avoided each other's eyes. We both still wanted more from her son than he wanted to give either of us. Dumb women, I thought. From now on I go after music, not men.

"He didn't mention anything," Twilah said airily. Proudly. A wave of jealousy swept over me. She talks to Greg and I don't. She's proud that I'm not important enough for him to mention.

I studied the keyboard, looked deep into my jealousy, and let it go. I felt Greg recede. I'll never win that one. Neither will she, he'll keep all of us at arm's length. I began a slow, cautious warm-up with a G Major scale. Tested the keyboard as if I were testing reality. The touch was loose, the sound mushy. It wasn't the best piano in the world, but it was workable.

"Do you want me to sight-read Brahms?" I asked, fingering the volume she'd placed on the music rack.

"That would be a waste of our time," said Twilah. "What are you working on in Bellingham?"

I waited before answering, trying to judge her motive for asking.

"Oh, for Heaven's sake, Virginia, I'm not spying on you and your Bellingham teacher. Focus. Focus on the music."

"This music is a story," I said, hesitating. "It even has chapter titles."

"Music is not story," Twilah said. "Music is always and only music."

"Well, Bach called it 'The Journey.'"

"I don't think I know that one."

"The chapter titles are in German."

"Music is neither German nor English," she said. "And there are no chapters."

"The words are German."

"Well, of course the words are German. Bach was German. Spare me words, Virginia. Play the music. Do you have it from memory?"

And so I played. I began the way I practiced, thinking of Bach's subtitle, 'The Departure,' and further sections: 'The friends plead: 'Remain with us,' 'They describe the dangers in foreign lands,' 'Sorrow and Regret,' 'Farewell,' 'The postillion comes,' and finally,

'Pleasant Journey,'

I couldn't drop old habits and so I stamped the opening passages with a thick layer of personal meaning. Hadn't I experience 'departure'? Been begged to 'remain'? Been warned about 'dangers'? Experienced 'sorrow and regret' before saying 'farewell'?

Twilah stopped me. "Forget about stories, Virginia. Forget about words. Forget about yourself. Bach has already done the work for you. Pay attention to the sounds you're making. Follow your fingers. Feel the muscles in your hands and arms. Let the pedal push into the sole of your foot."

I advanced on the next section and tried to drop the narrative; to stop illustrating ideas; to stop thinking. Noted the fingering and the logic of fingers. Heard the loud-and-soft dynamics. Became aware of the Sunday School piano thumping along; the pedal squeaking. Was conscious of hammers striking strings and yellowed old keys being depressed into their dusty beds.

For a short while I succeeded. I was here playing the piano. That was all. That was all Twilah expected. That was all Bach wanted. Nothing further was needed from me. I was complete. Absent and present at the same time.

47

And so I was drawn to High Street again: to Hilliard. At the beginning of July, I moved back into the old hotel. In my rooms, in the studio that Marguerite Cleary had created with her intelligence and strength, was shelter, yet not too much shelter. Warmth, but not too much warmth. As long as I lived here I would be a little chilly; I would be a little lonely. And then, like Twilah before me, like Marguerite Cleary, like Arturo's uncle who left as surely as the others—though he was carried out—like innumerable guests, lodgers, renters before me, I would leave; make myself absent from the old hotel; make myself present in a new place.

For hadn't Hilliard come apart and put itself together in a new shape? And wouldn't it do so again? The world was constantly coming apart and being put together, over and over. They will build another ship. A dried starfish will be removed from the stairstep while down at the harbor, under the dock, a new starfish is regenerating a lost arm.

Weren't Twilah and Arturo poised momentarily in Hilliard before their chunk of life broke off from the northwest edge of the continent and attached itself far away onto the Central American isthmus? Hadn't Greg pulled away from me and left me to my ambition? Hadn't I torn myself off from Seattle like a piece of bread from a loaf?

And don't my children wake up every morning to a new world?

About the Author

Marlene Lee has worked as a court reporter, teacher, instructor, and writer. A graduate of Kansas Wesleyan University (BA), University of Kansas (MA), and Brooklyn College (MFA), she currently tutors in the Writing Center at the University of Missouri. She has published numerous stories, poems, and essays. The Absent Woman, her debut novel, is set in Washington State where she lived in Seattle and had a sailboat in Anacortes.

The settings in Marlene Lee's work are almost characters in themselves. She would have difficulty choosing a favorite among the places where she has lived: small town and city, Kansas and Missouri, Northern and Southern California, Oregon and Washington, and New York City.

Marlene has two sons, four grandchildren, and has enjoyed her marriages until she didn't. She divides her time between a condo in Columbia, Missouri and an Upper West Side apartment in Manhattan.

http://marlenelee.wordpress.com/

CPSIA information can be obtained at www.ICGtesting.com
Printed in the USA
LVOW060100300413

331405LV00003B/71/P